FAIRFORD AFFAIRS
BOOK 4

ELEVATING
Eve

BAY SINCLAIR

To Bill and Paula, for supporting me through every step of my own personal renaissance.

And to Jason, who deserves infinite dedications.

CHAPTER 1
Jonathan

Jonathan scanned the architectural plans and financial statements spread across his desk and sighed. What a clusterfuck. Closing his eyes, he tried, without success, to massage away the band of pain squeezing his forehead like a vise.

Fairford Manor was starting to fall apart. The weird thing was that Jonathan couldn't even bring himself to be upset about it. Perhaps because it wasn't crashing down around him . . . more like it had begun to fray a little at the edges. While pulling on any of the loose threads wouldn't exactly destroy what he and the others had built here, it would never look the same either.

Revenues were way the fuck down. They'd already sunk millions into a new construction project that, so far, produced little more than a permanent stress headache. And though guest satisfaction remained remarkably high for a resort—let alone one that specialized in fulfilling their guests' deepest, darkest BDSM fantasies—it was starting to drop ever so slightly.

Not that it surprised Jonathan.

For its first five years, all the Manor's Doms provided around-the-clock experiences for each and every guest. Total immersion in the fantasy. A solid week in the sexiest dream imaginable. But now . . . with more and more of them falling in love and pairing off, change became the only option.

Or at least the only option with any chance of long-term success.

At the end of the day, that was Jonathan's number one job at the Manor. Keep it all together and inexorably moving forward, no matter what speedbumps or roadblocks got in the way.

A knock sounded on his office door. Jonathan straightened in his chair and arranged his features into a look of polite apathy. "Enter."

Jonathan held back a groan when he saw who walked through the door. "Please don't tell me there's another issue."

Frank Talley's answering grin did nothing to reassure Jonathan. The man owned the construction company currently three months behind schedule on the Manor's expansion project, and he donned that same phony expression no matter what news he planned to deliver.

"Unfortunately," Talley started, and Jonathan didn't bother stopping his groan this time. Why did more than half this fucker's sentences start with that word? Talley pursed his thin lips. "I can come back later if this is a bad time."

"Sorry, I'm having a rough day. Just lay it on me."

Talley lifted his eyebrows in that irritatingly superior way of his. "As you wish. The tile you chose for the bathrooms has been discontinued."

"Of course it has." Couldn't a single thing go right with this project? "Can we buy out whatever they have left in stock?"

There was that fucking smile again. For fuck's sake, why did he ever agree to hire this guy? "I checked on that, but unfortunately, we'd only be able to finish eleven of the bathrooms if we went that route. If that's how you'd like to proceed . . ." His tone made it very clear he thought it was a bad idea.

Yeah, well, no shit. Jonathan was perfectly capable of determining that on his own. "No, I still want them all to match." The twenty new guest rooms needed to be so perfect that no one minded staying in the new building instead of the main Manor house. He and the other partners had envisioned them as identical spectacles of luxury, and he refused to compromise on that vision.

Jonathan rubbed at his forehead again, willing his stress headache to disappear. No chance of that happening anytime soon.

"I anticipated you'd feel that way." Smugness dripped from each word, as if it was some great accomplishment to guess Jonathan would keep the opinion he'd already strongly expressed. "My assistant should be along shortly with new samples for you to review."

As if his words had summoned her, another knock sounded on the office door. "Enter," Jonathan said, voice a good deal kinder this time.

Jonathan did his level best to act as if nothing of note happened when Eve shuffled sideways through his door, a large box gripped in both hands. But the truth of the matter was, she took his breath away every goddamn time he saw her.

She had a face that should inspire artists to launch another Renaissance—perfect cheekbones, the most kissable lips he'd ever seen, a jawline he wanted to trace with his tongue. But it was that exceptionally thick, shiny, coffee brown hair that he literally dreamed about. He wanted to release it from her ever-present ponytail and run his fingers through it.

Wrap it around his fist and tug to expose her throat.

He wanted to touch her. Feel every inch of her softness and find all her hard edges. Discover her body's deepest secrets, always hidden beneath shapeless mom jeans and oversize shirts with her company logo on them.

Not that her outfit choices surprised him, given the amount of time she spent traipsing through the construction site, keeping an eagle eye on every aspect of the project. Meanwhile, Talley was all bluster and grandstanding in his immaculate, ill-fitting suit.

Without so much as a thank you, Talley yanked the box out of her hands. "You sure took your time."

Though he murmured the words, Jonathan had no trouble hearing them. A wave of anger rose from his belly up into his chest. "Respectfully, Mr. Talley, it's pretty obvious she did nothing of the kind."

Talley's eyebrows shot up again, and for once, he looked surprised rather than arrogant. "I beg your pardon?"

Gesturing in Eve's direction, Jonathan went on in the same clipped tone. "Look at her. Her skin is flushed. She's out of breath." Not something he'd expect for someone in such fantastic shape and on a mild day. He looked into her eyes—took in the shock and gratitude there. "You ran up both flights of stairs, didn't you?" He'd turned one of the spare rooms on the third floor into his private office when the expansion project began.

Her big brown eyes shifted toward her boss warily. But then she swallowed and stood up a little taller, meeting Jonathan's gaze again. "Yes, Mr. Hale, I did." Cheeks turning a deeper shade of red, she looked down toward her feet. "Sorry," she mumbled in Talley's direction.

Talley ran a hand over his flushed face, trying to hide his embarrassment. "No, I should be the one apologizing." He cleared his throat, as if the words got stuck there. "Sorry, sweetie. I'll make it up to you later."

Sweetie?

What the actual fuck? Six months he'd worked with Eve and Talley on this project. Half a year, and never once did he get the impression they were anything other than boss and assistant. If they were a couple . . .

No, Talley was well into his sixties, with the iron gray hair and wrinkles to prove it. And frankly, he was an asshole. Someone as sweet and stunning as Eve wouldn't go for *that*.

Would she?

The box hit his desk with a *thud*, yanking him out of his spiraling thoughts. "It would be good if you could make a decision by tomorrow," Talley said, still sounding as if he'd just sucked on a lemon. "To avoid any further delays."

Jonathan resisted the urge to roll his eyes. That made it sound like he and the other Manor partners caused the delays, which couldn't be further from the truth. "I'll do my best."

"Well, I'm afraid I'm needed elsewhere." Talley inched toward the door, not meeting anyone's gaze. "Eve, answer any questions he has about the tiles." With that, he shot out of the room as if the antique Persian rug was on fire. The fucking coward.

Eve let out the tiniest of sighs, staring at the closed door with disappointment in her eyes and deep frown lines around her mouth.

No, disappointment wasn't the right word. Every inch of her screamed defeat.

"Let's look at these tiles, shall we?" Jonathan said, trying to sound

4

cheerful rather than pissed off. If he could do anything to brighten the poor woman's day, he'd do it without question.

Eve's gaze lingered on the door for a few more seconds. Then she plastered a smile on her face and turned fully toward the desk. "There are some truly beautiful options here, Mr. Hale," she said, a perkiness to her voice that rang as false as a thousand-dollar bill. "I think we'll find something you love even more than the original tile."

He had his work cut out for him.

They'd narrowed it down to three tiles over the course of the last hour. Unsurprisingly, Eve knew every imaginable detail about all the tiles in the box—a profound attention to detail Jonathan had come to expect from her. He'd yet to find a single aspect of the project she couldn't talk about with near-encyclopedic knowledge.

No wonder she managed the site and crew instead of Talley.

"I can't tell you how much I appreciate your expertise. You've been a godsend these last six months." Jonathan studied her as he spoke, taking in the subtle shift in her posture and dilation of her pupils. Beautiful. So incredibly beautiful. She blossomed under praise.

And she was absolutely fucking starved for it.

"I'm so glad I can be of service," she said, blushing.

"It'll definitely be one of these." Jonathan ran his fingertips over the three remaining samples for at least the hundredth time. "I'll talk to my partners and get our final decision to you by ten AM."

She smiled, and this time it reached her eyes. Though her shoulders remained far too tense for his liking, he'd managed to loosen her up quite a bit since Talley left. "I look forward to hearing from you in the morning, Mr. Hale."

Jonathan snorted. "Eve, you've seen me naked. I think it's time you finally start calling me Jonathan, don't you?"

Laughter burst out of her, and she clamped a hand over her mouth, as if to keep any more sound from escaping. "I, uh . . ." Her cheeks turned a deep crimson, and she began twisting the heavy gold ring on her right middle finger around and around—a nervous habit he'd witnessed countless times in the last six months. "I didn't realize you knew I saw you."

Saw him? Fuck, she didn't just see him. She watched an entire scene out by the pool—first punishing his guest, and then giving her a pair of orgasms so explosive she slipped into subspace for half an hour.

Jonathan had seen Eve eating lunch in one of the garden's many little alcoves before the festivities began. Part of his brain insisted he take his guest inside. Though the construction crew knew exactly what kind of establishment they were working for, that didn't mean they signed up to be kinky voyeurs.

The larger part of his brain—the one controlled by his dick, if he was being honest—told him to proceed as planned just to see how she'd react. And sweet Christ, he wasn't disappointed. Eve stayed for the entire scene, hardly blinking as she took in every single detail.

With a smile he feared was a little too wolfish, Jonathan said, "Please don't be embarrassed. Voyeurism is not only allowed at the Manor. It's encouraged."

Eve turned her head away, trying to hide her smile of pleasure. "I'll keep that in mind." Her voice came out quite a bit lower than normal. "Until tomorrow morning, Mr. Ha—Jonathan." She took two steps toward the door, but then stopped, shoulders hunching forward again.

With his smile fading away, Jonathan asked, "Is everything okay?"

After a few seconds, she turned to face him again. She'd gone back to fidgeting with her ring, its square-cut emerald flashing in the lamplight. "There's something I think you should know."

Jonathan leaned back in his chair, trying to project an aura of calm to counteract her nervous energy. "I'm all ears."

Panic flashed in her eyes, and for a moment, he feared she would run off. But then she took a slow, steadying breath and forced herself to look him in the eyes. "Frank knew the tile you wanted was about to be discontinued. He knew before you even picked it."

Anger formed a ball in the pit of his stomach, but he did everything in his power to keep it from showing. "Why didn't he say something before now?"

"He waited to order it on purpose, hoping to get a big discount. That way his profit margin would be bigger." She chewed on her bottom lip for a few seconds. "You've been nothing but kind to me, and I thought you deserved to know."

Jonathan took several deep breaths through his nose, willing his emotions to subside. It wasn't Eve's fault her boss (slash boyfriend?) was crooked, and the woman obviously needed less anger in her life, not more.

"Thank you for telling me," Jonathan said, sounding almost like a robot to his own ears. "I'll talk to you in the morning."

She watched him for several seconds, chewing on that full lower lip again, her long lashes framing kind eyes filled with concern. Fuck, she was beautiful. He couldn't let himself get sidetracked right now, though, when he needed to find his business partners and start making some major decisions.

"Have a good night, Jonathan," Eve said in barely more than a whisper before she slipped from the room, closing the door silently behind her.

"Shit," he said, leaning back against the chair and closing his eyes. And he thought the project was a total clusterfuck before.

With a sigh, he fished his phone from his pocket and opened his eyes. Pulling up the group chat with all the partners—even Leo, their silent partner who lived in New York—he typed a quick explanation and asked what time they'd be available.

It was going to be a long-ass night.

CHAPTER 2
Eve

Could this building possibly go up any slower? Eve never worked on a project with so many stupid delays, and she'd been in this business for thirty goddamn years.

Well. Sort of. She helped her dad on jobsites every weekend and summer for as long as she could remember, until she grew old enough for him to hire properly. So yeah, maybe five-year-old-Eve's memories of the particulars were a little on the hazy side.

This job still sucked ass, though.

"Tommy, what on earth are you doing?" she asked, staring down her nose at one of their newest employees.

The gangly nineteen-year-old froze in place, the orbital sander in his hand stilling and falling silent. "Uh, I'm, uh . . ." He made random sounds for a few more seconds before Eve lost her patience.

"Did someone tell you to do that, Tommy?" she asked, her tone firm but kind.

"Um, yes ma'am. Mr. Talley did, first thing this morning." He frowned at her. "Is that bad?"

Eve held in a frustrated groan. Everywhere she turned, someone else was doing something either monumentally stupid, or a complete waste of fucking time. And almost without fail, they had been instructed to do so by none other than Frank. At this point, it almost felt like he *wanted* to fuck up the project.

Didn't mean the poor kid was to blame. "Go talk to Jake and figure out what he needs done." At least she could still count on her foreman to do things the right way. "And if Frank tells you to do anything else . . ." God, she couldn't believe she had to say this, but she didn't feel like she had a choice anymore. "Come find me or Jake before you start. I want all assignments going through us, understand?"

The idea of ignoring orders from the big boss clearly didn't sit well with Tommy. He fidgeted for a few seconds, not quite meeting her eyes anymore. "Yes ma'am, Ms. Hutchinson. Sure thing."

"Please stop calling me that," she said with what she hoped was a kind, not frustrated smile. Frank insisted everyone call him Mr. Talley, but she hated that shit. "Eve is just fine."

And he didn't even have to see me naked.

The thought popped into her head out of nowhere, and she was glad when Tommy scurried off in search of the foreman. It meant he didn't see how furiously she blushed. Because now all she could think about was how hot Jonathan was naked.

Not even hot—that was such a basic bitch of a word. Jonathan was the most intensely sexy human being she'd ever seen. And not just his body (though holy shit, what a body), but every single thing about him. How his gaze seemed to burn the surface of her skin. The way he moved, like a predator about to take down his prey. His deep, commanding voice, always so perfectly controlled, a world of emotion lurking just below the surface.

And, of course, the way he completely fucking *worshipped* that woman out by the pool. Holy fucking fuck. So much power as he yielded a thick leather strap against her bare flesh, never losing one iota of control. He comforted and soothed that beautiful woman, encouraging her through the pain until it melted away into pleasure.

Pain. Ecstasy. Escape.

Salvation.

It was everything she ever dreamed of.

Everything she wanted when she got involved with Frank all those years ago. What he convinced her he could give her.

She even believed him for a while. But somewhere along the line, things started to devolve. By the time their relationship turned into *this*, she'd been with him so long that she wasn't even sure how to go about leaving.

Fuck, she really did need to leave. But she'd lose literally everything she had in the process, and not just her home and security. Her father and Frank founded DHFT Construction a year before she was born, and virtually all her memories of her father involved this company. Losing her job would be like losing her dad all over again.

Besides, they had joint banking. She knew damn well Frank wouldn't let her take anything out of the accounts without a fight. Everything with him was a fight these days.

Jonathan, on the other hand, never allowed his anger to reach the surface. Even last night when she told him about Frank and those stupid fucking tiles.

That had been a mistake. She knew it even as the confession tumbled out of her mouth last night. Frank was going to go fucking ballistic when he found out.

She couldn't bring herself to regret it, though.

Maybe Jonathan wouldn't tell Frank where he got the info. Or maybe—

The thought died away as Frank stormed into the room, fury flashing in his eyes, his lips in a tight line.

Fuck, fuck, fuck. She needed to leave before things got out of hand. If she could just slip around back and head into town for a cup (or five) of coffee while he got his temper under control.

Too late. Frank spotted her across the room, and he took three long, way-too-loud breaths as he stared daggers at her. "I need to speak with you. Privately." Barely contained rage vibrated beneath the words.

Her heart pounded so hard and fast in her chest, it felt like a hammer slamming against her ribs. "I think we should talk after you've had a chance to calm down."

That was definitely the wrong thing to say. The expression that flashed across his face scared her so much she took several steps back, until a wall stud halted her progress.

Stalking across the room, Frank grabbed her upper arm in a painful grip. "Don't you dare embarrass me more than you already have," he hissed under his breath.

Eve knew exactly what would happen if she followed him outside. And she was fucking *done*.

"No." The single syllable seemed to reverberate through the room. "Let go of me."

Frank's eyes widened for the space of a heartbeat, before narrowing into tiny slits. "Everyone go outside and take a break," he said, raising his voice so people in the adjoining rooms would also hear.

"For God's sake." Eve rolled her eyes and tried to follow her crew out.

His grip on her arm tightened even more, making her gasp at the pain. "What the fuck do you think you're doing?" Frank spat down at her as the last of the workers filed through the door.

She looked pointedly down at his fingers wrapped around her arm, then back up into his eyes. "Same question."

"Don't get cute with me." He gave her arm a little shake, making her teeth rattle. "Do you have any idea how much trouble you caused me?"

Eve tried to yank her arm out of his grip, but his long, thick fingers were too strong. "I'm not doing this again," she said, trying to keep the fear out of her voice, without much success. "If you have a problem with me, talk to me about it. Don't grab me and yell at me and . . ." She let the sentence trail off. Neither of them acknowledged the rest of it out loud. Never. "This is exactly why I keep trying to get you to go to couples therapy with me."

"Fuck couples therapy." His standard response any time she brought it up.

She took a steadying breath, willing herself to stay calm and not give in to panic. "We need to learn how to communicate in a healthier way." She sounded cold and detached, like an AI voice relaying directions through a GPS app. "A *calmer* way."

"Stop." Danger lurked deep within that one word. "I don't know how you expect me to be calm when you went behind my fucking back and cost me twenty grand."

"Twenty grand?" Eve repeated, surprised. As far as she was

concerned, he was lucky DHFT wasn't fired from the project. That would've lost him a hell of a lot more than twenty thousand dollars.

Frank shook her again, and she ground her teeth together this time, so hard her jaw hurt. "Because of your big fucking mouth, Hale said he'd sue me if I didn't cover the difference between the old tile and the new one. And the prick picked the most expensive fucking tile in the box."

Some part of him had to know his shady actions caused this. Had to understand that when you do dishonest or illegal shit, sometimes it bites you in the ass.

When she looked into his eyes, though, she saw nothing there but raw fury, one hundred percent of it directed at her.

"I understand why you're angry," she said, using that Siri voice again. "But I couldn't stand by and let you screw these people over."

"So you decided to screw me over instead?" he demanded.

You screwed yourself over. It was right there on the tip of her tongue, but Frank was already a stick of unstable dynamite, fuse burning away. She had to proceed carefully if she wanted any chance of stopping the explosion. "My dad was an honest man. He'd turn over in his grave if he knew I didn't speak up."

"Your dad was an idiot." It felt like a physical blow, right in the stomach. "His stupid fucking *honesty* cost us a goddamn fortune. Or did you forget he left you nothing but debt? You should be thanking your lucky stars he died."

"Fuck you." She tried to dig her fingers beneath his and pry them away from her arm. "We're done, Frank. Let go of me right the fuck now."

He scoffed. "Oh, please. Don't embarrass yourself."

"*We're done,*" she repeated. "I don't ever want to see you again. Now let go of me before I scream."

Something new entered his eyes then. Shock, quickly replaced by a severe, almost obsessive possessiveness. That scared her even more than the anger did. "You're never leaving me." His voice was a low, dangerous growl that made the hairs on the back of her neck stand up.

Her instincts screamed at her to acquiesce. To just agree with him until this was all over and sneak away the first safe chance she got.

Her instincts could go to hell.

"That's not up to you, asshole. And I hope they do sue you. I'd rather see my dad's company fall apart than see it in your hands for another goddamn second." Leaning down, she bit the fleshy part of his hand just below the thumb.

"*Fuck!*" Frank yelled, yanking his hand away. The instant she straightened, the back of his hand slammed into her face.

Pain exploded across her cheek, behind her eyes, in her whole fucking head. *Motherfucking fuck.* It felt like her skull was shrinking, squeezing her brain so much it wanted to burst.

"You fucking bitch!" Frank snarled, drawing his hand back for a slap across the other cheek.

Cowering away from him, Eve put her arms up to protect her face. But the blow never came. After a few seconds, she peeked between her forearms, and her heart skipped a beat at what she saw.

Jonathan stood behind Frank with his hand wrapped around the older man's wrist. He bent Frank's arm back so far, it looked like only a tiny bit more pressure would snap bone.

A new sound hit her ears, and it took her several seconds to realize it was Jonathan's low, beautiful voice. Dropping her arms to her sides, she forced herself to focus on the sound until it changed into words—her name, repeated again and again.

"Yes?" she said, looking up into the man's intense brown eyes.

"Do you want me to call the police?" he asked, not even blinking as he watched her.

"I—what?" Her head felt unbearably fuzzy, blocking any coherent thoughts from forming. "The police?"

At that moment, Frank tried to whip around, aiming a wild punch in the vicinity of Jonathan's face. With a little sigh, almost like the attempt bored him, Jonathan easily blocked the punch, kicking Frank's legs out from under him. Frank hit the ground with a loud *thud* that made her wince.

"Yes, the police," Jonathan said, kneeling down and pinning Frank's hands behind his back. "He just assaulted you. Do you want to press charges?"

"I—I'm not—" Her mind raced. "I don't know."

Frank tried to buck Jonathan off his back, then gave up and half-shouted, "No, she doesn't want you to call the fucking police. Now get the fuck off me."

"Shut up," Jonathan said, not even glancing down at his captive. With his free hand, he pulled an honest-to-God handkerchief from his pocket, holding it out to her. "Here. You have blood on your cheek."

Blood? A hand flew up to her face before she could stop it, her fingertips gently prodding at the place where the heavy gold ring on Frank's finger had collided with her cheek. She gasped at the sudden burst of additional pain and pulled her hand away. Sure enough, her fingertips glistened red.

"Thank you," she said softly, taking the handkerchief and pressing it gently against her cheekbone.

"You ungrateful little slut!" Frank yelled, trying to twist his neck around to glare at her. "You had *nothing* after your father died. Every single thing you have is because of me, and this is how you repay me? After everything I—"

"Enough!" Jonathan's deeper, more powerful voice easily carried over Frank's. "Fucking Christ. Be quiet or I'll gag you."

Frank made a sound of disgust. "You'd like that, wouldn't you? You fucking perv. You get off on hitting women, but you have the fucking nerve to come at me about—"

Not bothering with a second warning, Jonathan yanked his tie off, balled it up, and shoved it into Frank's mouth. She watched her ex gag and splutter around the fine silk, clearly trying (and failing) to spit it out.

How had everything in her life gone so utterly and spectacularly wrong?

"Eve, I think you need to sit down." The words sounded strange, as if she heard them underwater. "Eve?"

She tried to meet his gaze, but she couldn't take her eyes off Frank's struggling, prone form.

"*Eve.*" A new sharpness in his voice snapped her out of it.

"Yes, Mr. Hale?"

"Sit down." It wasn't a suggestion anymore. "You look like you're about to pass out."

She plopped ungracefully onto the floor, hugging her knees to her chest.

"Good girl." He pulled his cellphone from his jacket pocket, holding it up for her to see. "I'm going to make one of two phone calls. I'm either calling the police, or I'm calling one of my partners so he can escort this piece of shit off my property. Your choice."

God, she just wanted this to be over. For Frank to be out of her life once and for all, and to find somewhere quiet to curl up and cry for the foreseeable future.

But when she looked down at him, everything changed. His expression held no regret, no fear. Not even a hint of pleading lurked in his eyes.

Frank Talley looked like he wanted nothing more than to wrap his hands around her neck and squeeze as hard as he could.

Revulsion coursed through her body, making her feel physically ill.

It wasn't the first time he'd hit her.

But it would sure as fuck be the last.

"I want you to call the police," she said, voice little more than a whisper.

Jonathan's small smile of approval washed over her, filling her cold, numb body with warmth. Unlocking his phone, he dialed 911 and hit send. Just before he brought the phone up to his ear, he looked her in the eye and once again said, "Good girl."

Her breath caught in her throat.

Just two simple words.

With the power to change her entire world.

CHAPTER 3

Jonathan

Hours later, Eve sat huddled in a leather armchair in his office, a white knitted blanket wrapped around her shoulders. A soft knock sounded on the door, and Zach Potter peeked his head in without waiting for an invitation.

"I brought her some tea," the Manor's receptionist said, keeping his voice low. Pushing the door open a little more, he held up a silver tray with a steaming mug, a few types of sugar, and a silver spoon.

"Thank you," Jonathan said, motioning for him to come all the way into the room. "That's very kind of you."

Zach always took it upon himself to take care of everyone, staff and guests alike. He'd stayed at the Manor for hours past his usual quitting time, for the sole purpose of bringing Eve some tea once the police finally left. The man had the biggest heart of anyone Jonathan had ever met.

He shuddered to think what the Manor would be like without him —not a thought he could bear considering for more than a second. Less than a year ago, Jonathan feared Zach was on the verge of quitting. Thank fuck that crisis had been averted.

The fact that Zach's chaotic journey to find happiness had placed

Eve in his path only just occurred to him. Wasn't that an interesting thought.

Laying the silver tray on the end table next to Eve, Zach asked, "Is there anything else I can get you, honey?"

She shook her head, not looking up. "Thank you," she murmured, taking the mug. She cupped it in her hands, the steam wafting gently over her face as she took a single, tiny sip.

Christ, what a day. The poor thing had to be exhausted.

Two police cruisers arrived twenty minutes after Jonathan called, quickly taking Frank into custody. They pulled the gag out immediately, tossing Jonathan's ruined tie onto the ground and giving him a look that said, *Really?*

He had exactly zero regrets on the subject. Especially after Frank started screaming a string of expletive-laden insults as they dragged him away.

Eve looked so fucking fragile as she held her hands over her ears, attempting to block out the hateful words. It hadn't improved as the police asked her questions, two men towering over her as she struggled to speak through her tears.

Relief washed through Jonathan when a third officer—a woman this time—ordered the others to step back, then sat down beside Eve on the floor. "We'll take this at your pace," the woman promised. "Let me know when you're ready."

Eve rallied after that, drying her tears away with one hand, the other once again pressing the bloody handkerchief against her cheek. The strength it took to answer all the officer's questions after what she just went through took his breath away.

She'd need that strength to make it through to the end of this process, especially if Talley took this to court instead of taking a plea. Jonathan made a mental note to reach out to his lawyer first thing tomorrow.

Now here they were, nestled in the safety and peace of his office. She watched over the rim of the mug as Zach all but tiptoed back out into the hallway, closing the door behind him with barely a sound.

"I like him," she said softly, still looking at the door. "He's always so nice to me. The way he talks to me . . . it makes me feel like I actually matter."

Her choice of words made his chest ache. Not that it surprised him. A guy like Talley would do everything he could to make a woman feel less than. Miniscule. Worthless.

Anything to keep her under his thumb.

"You matter to more than just Zach," he assured her, trying to keep the pity out of his eyes. That was the last thing she needed right now. "We all figured out you're the real brains behind this project in less than a week. Talley is a fucking buffoon."

That made Eve chuckle, which he filed away as a win. He desperately wanted to get that haunted look out of her eyes.

Her humor faded as quickly as it arrived, and she stared down at the mug now resting on her lap. "I'm sorry I caused you so much trouble."

Jonathan moved to the chair across from hers, perching on the edge of the seat. He leaned forward, his forearms resting on his thighs, so their eyes would be level. "You haven't caused any trouble at all, Eve. The only thing I'm upset about is that you got hurt. That I didn't get there fast enough to keep it from happening." After a moment, he felt compelled to add, "I didn't tell him you were the one who told me about the tiles."

Her head jerked up in surprise, her brown irises seeming to shine almost gold in the light pouring through the windows. "You didn't?"

"No," he assured her. In fact, he'd spent half the night on the phone with two of his partners, Leo and Aiden, trying to figure out the best way to confront Talley without even hinting at his source. "I did everything I could to keep you from getting into any kind of trouble." He ran a frustrated hand through his hair. "Obviously, I failed."

Eve lifted a tentative hand toward her injured cheek, her fingertips not quite touching the battered flesh. "Then how did you know to come rescue me?"

Jonathan sucked in a sharp breath at her words, though he tried to cover it up with a small cough. Something about the way she said that mesmerized him, but he couldn't put his finger on what.

Pushing that puzzle to the back of his mind to work out later, he said, "I watched Talley through my office windows after he left. I wanted to see what he'd do. When I saw him go into the new building, and then everyone but you came rushing out looking worried, I knew something was wrong."

A smile played at the edges of her beautiful, full lips. "Thank you. For everything you did today." She met his gaze for only a moment before looking back down at her lap. "I know I must seem pitiful. Just standing there while he . . ." She let the sentence trail off with a sigh.

"Was this—" He paused, considering the best way to word this. He wanted to be as kind as possible. "Has he ever hit you before today?"

Her shoulders hunched forward, and he immediately regretted asking the question. What a stupid fucking thing to do.

She surprised him, answering in a voice so soft he leaned forward to better hear her. "He didn't used to. Not like this, anyway. But the last couple years, he's changed. A lot."

"What do you mean, *not like this*?" Jonathan's brows drew together as he tried to work it out.

A blush colored her lovely, pale skin, rising up from her neck and spreading across her cheeks. Then she surprised him even more by smiling.

Beautiful.

"You know what you do?"

"What I do?" he repeated.

Her smile broadened, grew almost wicked. "What I saw you doing out by the pool."

All the pieces finally clicked together for him. "Ah," he said, his heartbeat kicking up a few speeds. "He used to be your Dom?"

She looked up at him through her lashes, and it took all his self-control not to grab her and haul her onto his lap. That look in her eyes drove him fucking wild. "Sort of," she said after a few moments. "I don't think it was exactly the same, though. He was always a lot harsher than you were. And the ending was completely different."

Jonathan remembered his scene out by the pool a couple of months ago. The one Eve had seen. How he'd given his guest two mind-shattering orgasms after her punishment, wringing every last bit of pleasure out of her body as she screamed.

"Completely different?" he repeated, arching a brow. "As in, you didn't come?"

Her eyes met his for a moment, and the raw lust he saw there stole all the air from the room. But then it was gone, and he couldn't help thinking he'd imagined the whole thing. Wishful thinking on his part, perhaps.

"No, I didn't." She twirled her emerald ring around her finger, staring down at her hands again.

"Ever?" The idea horrified him.

The thick gold band twisted faster and faster. "I mean, I did sometimes," she said, embarrassment filling the words. "When we were having regular sex. Just not, you know, after punishments."

Red hot anger spiraled out from the center of Jonathan's chest. And he thought he hated Talley before. "Eve, I need you to look at me for a minute, and really listen to what I have to say."

Her gaze snapped to his, finally remaining there for more than a handful of seconds. "Is something wrong?" she asked, frowning.

"What you're describing isn't a real Dom/sub relationship."

Eve blinked a few times, confusion in every inch of her expression. "I don't understand. What else would it be?"

Fuck, he was doing this all wrong. Running a hand through his already messy hair, he tried to think of a better way to explain. "Did you have any choice in the punishments?" he asked.

Her frown deepened even further. "Why would I have a choice? They were punishments."

"But did you have a safeword?" He needed her to understand this. "Could you stop him if you wanted to?"

She opened her mouth to answer, but then closed it again, staring off into space with a deep line between her brows.

"Talk to me," he urged. "Tell me all of it."

"I did have a safeword," she said, voice quiet and hesitant again. "But I only ever used it once."

Jonathan had a feeling he knew where this was going. "Why didn't you use it after that?"

"He just . . ." She let the sentence trail off as she wiped a solitary tear from her uninjured cheek. "He got so angry when I said it. He wouldn't talk to me or even look at me for a whole week afterward, like I was invisible. It was fucking awful." Her voice shook by the end.

His heart was breaking for the woman. "So you let him do whatever he wanted to do to you after that, because the silent treatment was even worse," he said as gently as he could.

Nodding, Eve wiped away several more tears.

"That isn't a real Dom/sub relationship," he told her again, hating the pain and confusion filling her eyes. "Talley was abusing and emotionally manipulating you, and there's *zero* place for that in a healthy BDSM relationship."

Eve closed her eyes and took a series of slow, deep breaths. At first, her lower lip and hands shook. But eventually they stilled, and she reopened her eyes. "I didn't know," she admitted. "He told me that's how it works."

A creeping suspicion wiggled its way into the back of his mind. "How old were you when you and Talley started dating?"

"Nineteen." Sighing, she added, "Frank was forty-six."

Disgust roiled in his stomach. It must have shown on his face, too, because she sounded defensive when next she spoke.

"I know what you're thinking, and you're probably right. I never should've gotten involved with someone so much older in the first place. But my dad had just died, and my whole life was falling apart, and Frank . . ." She sighed. "I don't know. He made everything make sense again."

How did this keep getting worse? "Taking advantage of a grieving young woman like that is—"

"No, it wasn't anything like that." Crimson painted her cheeks as soon as the words left her mouth. "I mean, I'm not trying to defend him or anything. Fuck him. But he wasn't just some random old asshole taking advantage of me."

Jonathan had a hard time believing that, but he motioned for her to keep talking. The least he could do was listen.

"I've known Frank my whole life. He and my dad were business partners. That's what DHFT stands for—Dennis Hutchinson and Frank Talley. Frank was all I had left after my dad died. He took care of me when no one else would. The falling for each other part . . . that just sort of happened on its own."

Jonathan's hands fisted of their own accord, and he ground his teeth together so hard he heard a rough, scraping sound. "How old are you, Eve?" he asked, doing everything in his power to keep the fury out of his voice.

She frowned, but promptly answered, "Thirty-five."

That surprised him, though he did his best not to let it show in his expression. She didn't look a day over thirty to him—not with that perfectly smooth, pale skin. "Any children?"

Sadness flitted through her eyes. "No. Frank said he'd be a senior citizen by the time they got to college, and he didn't want that."

"But you did?"

She nodded, slowly. "I always saw myself as a mom. But some things just aren't meant to be."

"Imagine you had a child. A daughter. And she was nineteen right now."

That line appeared between her brows again. "Okay . . ." she said, drawing out the word.

"Now imagine you pass away unexpectedly," Jonathan said, some real urgency in his voice. He felt a desperate need to help her see this the way he did. "Your daughter is beside herself with grief. And some man you work with, more than twice your daughter's age, shows up to comfort and take care of her, and then starts dating her while she's still grieving."

Eve opened and closed her mouth a few times, no words managing to make it past her lips.

"This girl is a teenager. Legally an adult, sure, but in all the ways that really matter? Maturity? Experience? Hell, even brain development. She's still a kid. And now she's a grieving kid. Do you really think any decisions she made right then would be good ones? That any relationship she started in that state could ever be healthy?" He paused a few moments to let all that sink in. "Is that what you'd want for someone you loved?"

Burying her face in her hands, Eve started to sob.

Jonathan launched himself across the short distance separating them, pulling her up out of the chair and into his arms. "It's all right," he said softly, hands hovering just above the surface of her back. The last thing he wanted was for her to feel she didn't have a choice to pull away —like she wasn't in total control of her own body. "It's not your fault. None of this was your fault."

He whispered the words again and again as her tears soaked through his shirt. He'd keep saying them as long as it took for her to start believing them.

CHAPTER 4

Eve

"Are you sure about this?" Eve hugged herself as tightly as she could. It did nothing to make the fear pulsing in time with her heartbeat go away.

Jonathan put a reassuring hand on her shoulder. "I'm positive. He's not being released until noon today."

Frowning, she started to ask how he could possibly know that. But he easily guessed her next question.

"My friend Nell knows someone at the Fairford Police Station. She had a similar sort of situation with an ex of hers about a year and a half ago, and she and the officer in charge of her case were friends by the end. Nell called her friend this morning and found out when Talley's being released."

Eve let out a long sigh. *Come on, you can do this.* It wasn't like she'd get a better chance to get all her stuff. And starting life over with literally nothing wasn't exactly on her to-do list. "Okay. Let's get this over with."

As they climbed out of Jonathan's Aston Martin, she tried not to touch anything unless she had to. The car had to be ridiculously expensive, and the thought of accidentally damaging the leather interior or scratching the paint terrified her. She shut the door so carefully, she wasn't even sure it latched.

When the trunk slammed shut behind her, she jumped at the loud *bang*. Jonathan clearly had no such fears about abusing his own car. "Okay, let's get everything you care about packed up as fast as we can." He had a stack of unassembled bankers boxes tucked under one arm, and the handles of at least a dozen large, mismatched duffel bags draped over the other. "Aiden will be here with his Land Rover in an hour, and we'll load everything up then."

Aiden was another of the ridiculously sexy Doms at Fairford Manor, and the only one she dealt with as much as Jonathan. He and Jonathan were overseeing the expansion project together. Apparently, the guy used to renovate houses for a living, and even did a lot of the work restoring the main Manor building himself. She had a hell of a lot of respect for his skills—especially the way he kept so much of the old mansion's original woodwork.

"I really appreciate you both helping me," Eve said as she led the way up the walkway to the front door. Though for the life of her, she couldn't figure out why they would. It's not like she worked for them anymore. Frank may not have had a chance to officially fire her yet— hard to do that from a jail cell. But the Manor's lawyer drew up the papers to terminate the contract with DHFT first thing that morning.

Jonathan followed her up onto the large farmer's porch. "I wish you'd take us up on our other offer," he said for the third time since they left Fairford an hour and a half ago.

Repressing the urge to snap at him, she unlocked the front door, stepping into the house she'd shared with Frank for the last eleven years. She didn't say a word as she started up the staircase—what was the point? She'd already told him twice that, while she appreciated the offer, she didn't feel comfortable staying at the Manor while she figured out her next move. Badgering her about it wouldn't change anything.

"I'm sorry," he said as he followed her upstairs. "I know I shouldn't pressure you. I won't bring it up again."

"I, um . . . thank you." It came out almost like a question. Why had her heart just skipped a beat?

They made it halfway down the second-floor hallway before it finally dawned on her. Jonathan *apologized*. He admitted he'd done something wrong and pledged not to do it again.

Fury ran through her body hot and fast. How fucked up was it that a simple apology could affect her like that? Her relationship with Frank was even shittier than she thought.

"Most of my stuff is in here," she said, leading him into her office. Frank had very particular taste and didn't want her things cluttering up his overall design for the house. He didn't even like sharing the master bedroom's walk-in closet with her.

Can I have Red Flags for two hundred, Alex?

"You pack up the desk," she said, trying to focus on the task at hand. There would be plenty of time later to unpack the nearly two decades of bad choices she'd made. "I'll work on the closet."

With a nod, Jonathan settled into her desk chair, assembling the whole stack of white and blue boxes. She stared at his hands for way too long, entranced by the confidence and efficiency of his long fingers. Afraid he might think she was a giant weirdo, she forced herself to turn away, grabbing a couple of the duffels and heading into the small walk-in closet.

Get a fucking grip, Eve. Was she seriously getting turned on by the way he put cardboard boxes together? Was she that starved for a real connection with another person?

Besides, she literally just got out of the relationship from hell. Yesterday. Maybe she could wait at least forty-eight hours before she started lusting after someone else.

She stopped herself from snorting at the last second, not wanting to have to explain the sound to Jonathan. But seriously, who was she kidding? She started lusting after Jonathan the second she laid eyes on him last October.

Focus, damnit. Unzipping the first duffel bag, she began yanking shirts off their hangers and shoving them inside. She had one hour to pack up sixteen years of her life. She'd worry about the wrinkles later.

The Fairford Inn was an old, three-story brick building in the heart of downtown Fairford.

Technically, all of downtown Fairford was in "the heart." The whole thing was comprised of a single long street, lined on both sides with shops, restaurants, and small businesses.

Eve had fallen in love with the tiny town the first time she and Frank drove through it on their way to the initial consultation with Jonathan and his partners. It felt surreal to be living here a mere six months later.

"Here's the last of it," Jonathan said, carrying the final two bags of clothes into her room on the inn's second floor. They'd propped the door open with a box full of random knick-knacks while they moved everything inside from the Land Rover. Since Eve was currently the only guest, she wasn't super worried about someone stealing her stuff.

She peered over his head as he bent to put the bags in the closet, stacking them on top of those already covering the floor. "Where's Aiden?"

"He had to head out. He has a guest arriving at the Manor in a couple hours." Jonathan straightened back to his full height as he spoke, and she tried not to drool as she watched. The man had to be six-one or six-two, every inch of his tailored suit perfectly filled out by his lean muscle. Why he would choose a suit to help her move was beyond her, but in six months, she'd never seen him wear anything else.

Focus, she admonished again. But it was a lost cause. Watching Jonathan carry boxes all afternoon had her pussy aching.

What would it be like to sleep with a man like Jonathan? Would it feel as good as that woman by the pool made it look?

Hell, if it felt even half that good, it would be the best sex of her life.

It was way too soon to be thinking about jumping into bed with another man. She still had a fucking gash on her face from the last one, for fuck's sake.

But it had also been way too long since she felt good.

"All right, that should do it," Jonathan said, moving back through the doorway. He turned to face her just past the threshold, his gaze scanning the room. "I'm glad we managed to cram everything in here."

Eve's laugh came out a little too fast—a smidge too high. Fuck, she sounded like an idiot. Someone like Jonathan Hale only slept with poised, confident women. Of that she had no doubt. "It's not ideal," she said, fidgeting with her ring, then making herself stop a few seconds later. She hated that she did that every time she got nervous, but after so long, the habit would be impossible to break. "But it'll do until I can figure out where to go from here."

She'd be staying in Fairford for at least another couple of weeks until the partners figured out who to hire to finish the new building. On the drive back from Frank's house, Jonathan asked her to help the new team get up to speed on the project, since she knew all the details better than anybody.

Given the amount of money he offered for her assistance, she couldn't have refused even if she wanted to. She'd need that money while she searched for a new job.

After those few weeks were up, though, she had zero idea what came next—something she very much didn't want to think about right now. Not when her world had literally just been turned upside down and inside out.

God, she longed for anything to distract her from her churning thoughts.

"You have my number, and you know where to find me," Jonathan said, looking down at her with a little smile. "Take a few days to get settled in, and when you're ready, we can talk about next steps for the—"

Eve rocked up onto her toes and pressed her lips against his.

CHAPTER 5

Jonathan

F uck, fuck, *fuck*.

In an instant, Jonathan's dick was hard as fucking granite. All the basest instincts in his body told him to grab this stunning creature, bend her over the foot of the bed, and fuck her until the sun came up.

He placed his hands on her shoulders, pushing her away as gently as he could. "Eve," he said, hearing the regret filling his voice. "We can't."

The look of mortification on her kind, beautiful face sent guilt spiraling through him. "Oh, God." There was a panicked edge to her voice. "I'm so fucking stupid. I'm so sorry."

"Listen to me. It's not—"

She grabbed the door and flung it closed.

Jonathan winced as the door collided with his foot. He felt that impact through the fine Italian leather of his shoe.

Her wide eyes met his for one shocked second. Then she turned, hiding her face from him. "Please leave," she whispered, voice shaking with barely restrained tears.

"I promise I'll leave as soon as you hear what I need to say." The words sounded as soft and gentle as he knew how to make them. No way would he use his usual commanding Dom voice when he already felt like shit for taking away her choice to kick him out. But she needed to hear this. "I'm not rejecting you, Eve. I mean, look at you. I've wanted you since the moment I first saw you."

She drew in a sharp breath. Her hand shook as she pulled it away from the door, allowing him to open it the rest of the way. She turned to face him again, though she didn't quite meet his gaze. "Then why . . ." She couldn't seem to figure out how to finish the question.

Reaching out, Jonathan cupped her injured cheek with his hand, doing everything in his power to keep from hurting her. "I'm not going to do the same thing Frank did all those years ago."

Her mouth dropped open the tiniest bit.

"If, after all this is sorted out and you're back on your feet, you still want to do this, I would be more than happy to oblige." He'd be fucking ecstatic. "But I'm not going to take advantage of you when you're hurt and vulnerable."

She stared into his eyes for so long, desire radiating from her like a cat in heat, that his resolve almost weakened. *Almost.* But he'd never be able to forgive himself if he let anything happen tonight.

At long last, she let out a sigh. "Of course you're one of the noble ones." Disappointment filled her eyes, but her lips held the hint of a smile. "Not that I'm surprised. It's probably half the reason I'm so attracted to you."

"And the other half?" Jonathan asked, his own lips quirking upward.

"Your ass," she said, eyes scrunching up at the corners. "Definitely your ass."

He laughed as gratitude eased the guilt still lingering in the pit of his stomach. Thank God everything would be all right between them. He couldn't stand the thought of losing her before he even had her. "And here I thought it was my charming personality."

She smiled bigger than he'd ever seen from her.

And Christ, her smile was beautiful.

"Okay, Prince Charming," Eve said with an amused shake of the head. "Let me get some sleep so I can start getting my head on straight. I'll see you in a couple days."

Jonathan bowed low like a prince in an old black-and-white movie, loving the sound of her giggle. "My lady." He backed away from the threshold, letting her shut the door between them.

Fishing his phone out of his pocket, he pulled up his text thread with Leo and typed, *Sometimes being noble really fucking sucks.*

With a sigh, he dropped the cell phone back into his pocket and headed toward his car.

Jonathan buried his hands in his hair and groaned. He was back in his office on the Manor's third floor, trying to get some work done, but he couldn't concentrate.

"How did you know to come rescue me?" Fuck, he'd never get those words out of his head. An image popped into his mind then—Prince Charming in gleaming armor atop a pristine white horse, sword held aloft as he charged unwaveringly to save a damsel in distress.

Not just any damsel in distress. *Eve* in distress.

Reaching down, he pressed his knuckles roughly against his cock through his slacks, trying to get the damn thing to calm down. Since when did he have a savior kink? Hell, was that even a real thing?

Well, if it wasn't before, the pulsing in his cock made it awfully clear it was now.

"Oh, fuck it," he mumbled, fumbling with his belt. He wasn't getting any work done anyway.

He closed his eyes when he finally wrapped a firm hand around his dick. Eve's name tumbled from his lips as he squeezed, pumping his hand up and down the shaft.

The image of himself astride a charging steed popped back into his head, and this time he ran with it. The evil wizard was slain, and now he merely needed to climb to the top of the tower to claim his prize.

In his mind, the fantasy skipped ahead to the part where he opened the door to the highest room in the crumbling old castle.

Eve knelt in the center of the circular room, looking up at him with gratitude shining in her big brown eyes. "Thank you for rescuing me, noble prince." Her smile held a world of delicious promises. "From this day forth, I'm yours to command. What do you wish of me?"

He let his gaze travel downward, taking in her ample breasts, barely contained by the green silk dress she wore. Down farther still to her trim waist, cinched tight by a belt of shimmering gold. Then to her hands, resting on her lap, pressed together in supplication.

His princess looked so fucking beautiful on her knees.

Strolling lazily into the room, he took his time circling her, drinking her in. "Rise, my lady," he said at last, taking one of her small hands and helping her to her feet. "You say you're mine to command?"

She blinked up at him coyly. "Yes, my prince."

"And you swear to obey me in all things, no matter what I ask of you?"

"Yes, my prince," she purred.

He lifted his free hand to her face, brushing his fingertips along her cheekbone. "Good girl." Moving behind her, he began undoing the laces at the back of her dress, tugging them loose until the fabric slipped down her shoulders. "Bare yourself to me."

With a shudder of excitement, Eve got to work removing her clothing one piece at a time. She started with the belt made of gold discs, each circle of metal imprinted with the image of a blazing sun. The rest of the clothing followed quickly behind, until she stood before him in nothing but her skin.

Jonathan circled around her again, even slower this time. He wanted to memorize every single inch of her with his eyes, then do it all over again with his hands and tongue.

"Do I please you?" she asked, looking up at him through her lashes.

"Mmm," he answered, tracing down the length of her right arm with the tip of one finger, marveling in the softness of her skin. "Nothing has ever pleased me more."

A rosy blush colored her cheeks as she looked down—the pose demure, but her smile revealing her pleasure at his words. "Before we go any further, I must confess something." Despite the gravity of those words, the smile stayed firmly in place.

"Yes, princess?"

One small, pale hand drifted across her hip, inching toward her center. "I know I was meant to stay pure for my champion. But I've been waiting so long."

Jonathan's heart pounded in his chest as he covered her wandering hand with his own, stopping its progress. "Has my little princess been a bit naughty?"

She looked up at him with wide, pleading eyes. "Only because of my longing for you. Please say you'll forgive me?"

"Are you willing to earn my forgiveness?"

"I'll do whatever you ask," she answered, the words soft and smooth as velvet.

Jonathan's lips spread into a slow smile. "That's just what I wanted to hear." Leading Eve over to the bed, he bent her over the thick mahogany footboard, pushing her forward until the intricate carvings in the wood pressed against her thighs. "You will submit to me."

It was an order, not a question, but still she answered, "Yes, my prince."

Placing a hand on her lower back, he slid it down over the curve of her ass. "You will accept the punishment I deem appropriate, without a fight."

"Yes, my prince." It came out in a breathless rush.

Lifting his hand high, he brought it down against her with a loud crack.

Eve shouted in surprise, lurching forward as much as the unforgiving wood of the footboard would allow. "Please!" The single word came out as a high, keening wail.

"Yes, my lady?" It sounded smug even to his own ears.

"That's too hard," she said, hands fisting in the fine silk blanket covering her large bed. "I can't take it."

He rubbed the rosy mark his hand left behind on her pale skin. "You agreed to accept my punishment without a fight," he reminded her, squeezing hard enough to make her gasp.

Whimpering, she whispered, "Yes, my prince."

"Good girl. Now let's continue."

Without any warning, he brought his hand down twice more in quick succession, once on each cheek. Again, her body pitched forward, but she didn't beg him to stop this time. Instead, she buried her face in the blanket, letting the purple silk muffle her cries.

Jonathan smiled. His brave, submissive little princess. It was time for her spanking to truly begin.

He brought his hand down against her tender flesh in a steady

35

rhythm, spaced far enough apart for a burn to ignite beneath her skin, but each impact coming too soon for her to catch her breath. When administered correctly, a spanking was truly a work of art.

Jonathan was a master of his trade.

Her whole body shook with each heaving sob, her cries now far too loud for the silk to muffle them. But still she stayed in position, never once attempting to rise or moving her hands back to protect her burning skin.

He was so proud of her courage that he ended the spanking before he had originally intended. The previously pale skin glowed a bright red—not quite the deep crimson he wanted. But she had earned the reprieve.

"Was that your first spanking?" he asked, rubbing her bottom with gentle hands, trying to soothe the worst of the pain away.

It took her almost a minute to get her crying under enough control to answer. "Y-yes," she said, her voice catching. "Did I please you?"

"Oh, my sweet princess." He let one hand slide toward her core, fingers gently probing. She was ready for him, her arousal hot and slick against his skin. "You couldn't have possibly pleased me more." With that, he plunged two fingers into her pussy. They slid in easily, her wetness coating his fingers and dripping down onto his hand.

All she managed in reply was a low, drawn-out moan.

Freeing his cock at last, he lined it up with her entrance. "You're mine," he growled, grasping her hips with rough, possessive hands. "I'll make sure you never forget it." Then he plunged his hips forward, burying himself in her scorching heat.

"Fuck!" Jonathan yelled, throwing his head back as hot come spilled onto his hand and all over his slacks. He'd been so lost in the fantasy, he hadn't even realized he was about to tumble headfirst over the edge.

Letting his sticky hand fall to his side, he closed his eyes again and tried to catch his breath.

Jesus fucking Christ. What was this woman doing to him?

CHAPTER 6
Eve

I t only took Jonathan and Aiden a week to choose two potential construction companies to finish the new building. And good God, they were eager to land the job. At both consultations, the company owners fell all over themselves in their efforts to suck up to Jonathan and Aiden. Eve spent the whole time on the verge of death by second-hand embarrassment.

She could only imagine the exorbitant amount of money on offer to get the project back on schedule. No wonder the two men made such fools of themselves.

She waited in the study on the Manor's first floor while Jonathan and Aiden showed the owner of the second company out. Eve didn't think it was her place to have any say in the selection process, but when Jonathan insisted, she'd agreed to tag along for the meetings.

Hopefully they didn't pressure her into offering too many opinions, because she had a feeling they wouldn't like anything she had to say.

Only a few minutes ticked by on the carriage clock on the mantle before the men returned. "Thank God that's over," Aiden said, dropping unceremoniously into one of the overstuffed leather armchairs. "I thought he'd never stop talking. My next guest is arriving in less than an hour."

Jonathan took one of the remaining chairs with much more care, careful not to wrinkle his suit. "Let's not waste any time, then. What do you think?"

A contemplative look stole into Aiden's kind brown eyes. "It's tough to say," he said, speaking slowly as gears continued turning in his head. "I think both would do a good job. LGF might be the obvious choice—"

"Since they're cheaper," Jonathan supplied.

"Right. But Crane & Faber has a bigger team. I think they'd do the work faster." Aiden shrugged. "So it all depends on what's most important to us."

Eve sat perfectly still in her chair, careful to keep any sort of reaction off her face. Not her money, not her decision. She repeated that over and over in her mind.

"Agreed," Jonathan said with a thoughtful nod. "And given how far behind schedule we already are, I think it might be worth a little extra money to get us back on track."

Aiden considered that in silence for a bit, and she could practically see a pros and cons list written in his eyes. "It would make Remy happy."

That was certainly true. The Manor's Director of Event Planning emailed her at least once a week asking for updates on his shiny new event space. Or at least he *used* to email her once a week. She supposed someone at Crane & Faber would soon have that honor.

How unfortunate.

She almost said something. *Almost.* She pressed her lips together and stayed silent.

"So is that it?" Aiden asked, peeking at his watch and wincing. "Are we going with Crane & Faber?"

Jonathan started to answer, but then stopped himself, finally looking at her. "What do you think?"

Well, shit. A ball of dread formed low in her belly. "I don't really think it's my place to say."

Jonathan's expression made one thing perfectly clear—he wouldn't accept such a bullshit answer. "You've been in this business your entire life. I'm asking for your expert opinion."

"Aiden's also an expert. You already have his opinion." She knew it wouldn't work, but she had to try.

Gracing her with a kind smile, Aiden said, "My area of expertise is a little different. But I appreciate you saying so."

"God save me from stubborn men," she muttered, earning a frown from Jonathan and a chuckle from Aiden.

"You're the only one here being stubborn," Jonathan said, giving her his full Dom look for the first time ever, and holy mother of God, it was a good thing she was already sitting down. She felt weak in the knees.

With a steadying breath, Eve forced herself to stay calm. "It would make me uncomfortable to make a decision that could have a major financial impact on your business. I don't think it's appropriate."

"I'm not asking you to make the decision." Jonathan ran a hand through his perfect hair, knocking several strands out of place. "I just want your opinion."

He was really getting frustrated now, and all her experiences with Frank told her to give him what he wanted.

Fuck that.

She didn't think anything on the planet would make Jonathan react the way Frank did. And after sixteen years of being a total doormat, she couldn't resist the urge to poke the bear. "Well, as the saying goes, you can't always get what you want."

"Oh, for fuck's sake," Jonathan snapped. "Are you serious right now?"

A euphoric sense of power coursed through her, and a laugh bubbled up out of her throat. She clamped her teeth together, trapping the sound inside, but it was too late.

Something dangerous—and remarkably sexy—flashed in Jonathan's eyes. "Are you laughing at me?"

"Um." She looked to Aiden for assistance, but the man might as well have had a bucket of popcorn on his lap. He was too busy enjoying the show to come to her aid. "No?"

"No," he repeated, his voice a low growl. "I see." Standing, he crossed the space between them, until she had to crane her neck to see his face.

Fuck, he was tall. And this close, his scent seemed to surround her. *So. Damn. Good.* He had to be wearing the same cologne as last week, when he held her while she cried—woodsmoke and heather. It made her want to leap up and wrap herself around him.

"Now that I have your attention," he said, the look on his face making her pussy flutter, "let me make one thing perfectly clear. I told you I wouldn't take advantage of a hurt and vulnerable woman, and I meant it. But I'm an incredibly patient man. I can wait. So if you think you're getting away with something right now, think agai—"

"Neither," she blurted.

Jonathan's head jerked back in surprise. "Excuse me?"

Goddamnit. She didn't mean to say that. But the way he looked at her made the word fly right out of her mouth.

Oh, well. In for a penny, in for a pound.

"I don't think you should hire either of them. They both suck."

A range of emotions crossed Jonathan's face one after the other—shock, confusion, anger, frustration. At last, he looked over at Aiden, seemingly at a loss for words.

Aiden's eyebrows lifted slightly, and one corner of his mouth twitched. "Be careful what you wish for."

"That's all you have to say?" Jonathan demanded.

The other man only shrugged.

He rounded on Eve again. "You're just saying that to irritate me."

"No, I refused to tell you my opinion to irritate you." She resisted the urge to smirk. That wouldn't help her case. "Now I'm just doing what you asked me to do."

"But why wouldn't I hire one of them?" The muscles in his jaw ticked. "They're both well-known, established companies with hundreds of positive testimonials. I liked both of their presentations. They—"

"Of course you liked their presentations," Eve said, rolling her eyes. "You had your ass kissed for a solid four hours today. Who wouldn't like that?"

Jonathan's mouth dropped open. In all the months she'd known him, she'd never seen him look so uncomposed. This new side of him fascinated her.

Taking a step back, he pulled on the ends of his sleeves and the bottom hem of his jacket almost absently, as if he didn't realize he was doing it. "I have no idea what you're talking about," he said, trying to sound calm and in control again.

Arching her brows as high as she could, she crossed her arms and gave him a sardonic look. "I'm sure you don't. People have been kissing your ass for so long, you don't even know how to recognize it anymore."

Jonathan couldn't have looked more stunned if she spontaneously donned an ostrich feather tail and started doing the cancan.

Across the room, Aiden made a garbled choking noise and hurried over to the side table full of booze. His shoulders shook ever so slightly as he poured himself a drink.

"See?" Eve tilted her head in Aiden's direction. "He knows what I'm talking about."

"Hey, leave me out of this," Aiden said, unable to keep the amusement out of his voice. "I need to go get ready for my guest. Good luck." A deep amber liquid sloshed in his tumbler as he sauntered out of the room, throwing a fleeting smile over his shoulder when he shut the door.

They stared at each other, the tension in the room so heavy, the air felt too thick to breathe. It sent a thrill down her spine that she hadn't felt in decades.

"You're used to people doing what you tell them to do." She didn't bother phrasing it as a question.

He snorted. "Of course I am. I'm a professional Dom. That's literally my job."

"No, that's not what I mean," Eve said, shaking her head. "I'm not talking about your guests. I'm talking about everyone else."

Jonathan frowned, but he didn't answer.

"Everyone here defers to you," she said, tilting her head toward the door Aiden just exited. "Even your business partners. I noticed it the first day I met you all."

She could tell he wanted to deny it, but the truth was written all over his face.

"No one really challenges you anymore, do they?" Standing, she reached out a tentative hand, her fingertips brushing against his sleeve. "Doesn't that get boring?"

"You never challenged Talley at all," he shot back. "Didn't *that* get boring?"

Eve let her hand fall back to her side. "Boring isn't the word I'd use to describe it," she said softly.

Shame washed over his face, settling in his eyes. "I'm sorry. I shouldn't have said that."

"I stopped trying to stand up to Frank because everything always went to shit when I did." She didn't know why she felt a burning need to explain, but the words continued to pour out of her. "I couldn't leave. So I made things as easy for myself as I could."

"Why couldn't you leave?" It wasn't an accusation this time—just an honest question.

She looked down at her hands as she began fiddling with the heavy gold ring. "DHFT was all I had left of my dad. If I ended things with Frank . . . if I lost that job . . ."

"Oh, Eve." So much understanding and compassion filled those two words.

Blinking away tears, she tried for a nonchalant shrug. "By the time I realized how much of myself I gave up for him, there was hardly any of me left anymore. And look what I have to show for it. No job, no home, no anything. Just this." She held up her right hand.

"The ring was your dad's?"

She nodded, finally giving in to her tears.

Jonathan wrapped his arms around her, pulling her gently against his chest. "No wonder it's so important to you," he said as he traced a gentle pattern on her back. "But it's not the only thing you have."

Her laugh was bitter. "Oh, yeah. My life's just peachy."

"I mean it." He pushed her out to arm's length, waiting until she met his gaze before continuing. "You may not have your job at DHFT anymore, but you still have every single thing your dad taught you when you worked with him. You're the only person at that whole damn company I trusted to know the answer when I had a question. Did you know that?"

Emotion clogged her throat, keeping her voice trapped inside. She shook her head instead.

"That's why I wanted your opinion today. You know more about the construction business than anyone I've ever met." Reaching up, he brushed her tears away with his thumb. "And that's something Frank fucking Talley can't ever take away from you, no matter what company you work for."

God, she really wanted to kiss him now. She'd never wanted someone more in her whole life.

Soon, she promised her raging libido.

Stepping back, she took a moment to compose herself. "Thank you," she said when at last she had her tears under control. Her voice still shook slightly, but it would have to do. "That really means a lot to me. I hadn't thought about it that way."

"Don't let yourself forget it," Jonathan said, voice kind but firm. "I obviously didn't know your dad, but he must have been a hell of a man for you to admire him so much. A man like that would be proud of everything you've accomplished. He'd want you to be happy."

"Oh, God, I'm gonna cry again." She covered her eyes with one hand and took several deep breaths. "Change the subject before I completely lose it."

Without missing a beat, he asked, "Why do both companies suck?"

Eve smiled as her hand dropped back to her side. She couldn't help herself. "You don't give up, do you?"

"It's the first thing I could think of," he said with a rueful smile.

She rolled her eyes. Of course it was. "Okay, okay. You win. LGF is too small for the project. They'll hire a bunch of people really fast the second you give them their first check, but this is northern Vermont. They won't have a talent pool deep enough to get actual skilled laborers, and they'll have to take anyone willing to come all the way up here for the next several months. In the end, they'll do a piss-poor job, and it'll end up costing you a fortune to fix it."

Jonathan's eyes grew wider and wider the longer she talked. "Wow. Okay. LGF is out. What about Crane & Faber, though? They're the largest construction company in the region. They were on our short list the first time, in fact."

"Cole Faber is a decent guy, and he knows what he's doing. If it was him who came today, and he'd be overseeing the project, I'd have no objections."

"But?" he prompted.

"But Larry Crane is a raging alcoholic who can't keep his hands to himself when he's had too much to drink." She'd been at the receiving end of his drunken advances more than once at conferences over the years. The fucker. After the first time she put him on his ass, she never went anywhere alone when she knew he was around. "That's the last thing you want at a resort full of beautiful, half naked women. It's a lawsuit waiting to happen."

"Jesus." Jonathan raked a hand through his hair. "That's putting it mildly."

She sighed. "Sorry. I know you want to get a new crew in here as fast as possible."

"I want to get the *right* crew in here as fast as possible," he corrected. "Trust me, I appreciate the info. Is there anyone you would recommend?"

A few names popped into her head immediately. "Maybe." She'd need to do some research and make a couple phone calls first. "Let me think on it. I'll have some options in your inbox by tomorrow morning."

Jonathan's smile was more than a little smug once he finally got his way.

She wanted to kiss it right off his stupid, gorgeous face.

Soon, she told herself again. If he could be patient, so could she.

Enough lusting after someone she knew she couldn't have yet. She had a shattered life to piece back together. First step: find a new job.

Exhaustion had seeped deep into Eve's bones by the time she pulled into the parking lot behind her hotel. How was it that a difficult conversation drained her as much as a full day of labor on a jobsite, if not more?

Sighing, she climbed out of her car and headed around the side of the inn. As she rounded the final corner onto Main Street, she froze, her heart pounding like she was a rabbit caught in a fox's gaze.

Frank leaned against the brick wall between her and the door, looking down at his phone.

Shitshitshitshitshit.

Options ran through her mind in a rapid-fire procession.

One: confront him. Yeah, fuck no. She tried that already. The still-healing gash on her face proved she shouldn't try it again, at least not on her own.

Two: call Jonathan. She dismissed that idea even faster than the first one. It would take him twenty minutes to get here—maybe ten if he drove like a maniac. And the last thing she wanted was for him to get into an accident, especially when his arrival would be too late no matter what.

That left option three: turn around and run. And do what, exactly? Move to another hotel?

Go back to the Manor, her panicked brain insisted, and the thought calmed her ever so slightly. Jonathan wanted her to stay at the Manor anyway. He wouldn't object if she had to spend a night or two there.

Mind made up, she started to creep backward into the alley between the inn and the boutique clothing shop next door. That's when Frank finally decided to look up.

Their gazes locked, and she was back to being the goddamned rabbit. Every muscle in her body locked in place as her mind screamed impotently for her to turn tail and flee.

"Eve." He used that ultra calm, I'm-the-one-being-reasonable-while-you're-overreacting voice he always did after he screwed up big time. "Don't you think this has gone on long enough? It's time to come home."

Fuck. You.

She was so fucking sick of all the gaslighting. It had to stop.

Now.

Forcing herself to breathe in and out, she waited for her heart to slow, for some of the feeling to return to her limbs. Not trusting herself to make it to her car before he caught up with her—not when her legs felt like jelly beneath her—she moved toward Frank with slow, deliberate steps. If this had to happen, she wanted it to be on a public street, not in an alleyway or secluded parking lot.

"Frank," she acknowledged, trying for that same frustrating-ass tone he used. It sort of worked. "I know you already heard from my lawyer. I have nothing else to say to you."

Jonathan's lawyer had offered to represent her pro bono, and promised to be present during any future interviews with the police. So far, she'd only spoken to Tabitha via Zoom, but Eve liked the woman already. She somehow managed to have a no-nonsense attitude, getting straight to the facts, while also exuding a gentle kindness that set her at ease immediately.

In fact, Tabitha reminded her of that badass lady cop—the one who made the two male cops looming over her and barking questions fuck off and give her some space.

Lifting her chin into the air, Eve tried to walk past Frank and head inside. She expected him to reach out and stop her, but her skin still crawled when he did it.

With another deep breath, she forced herself to meet her ex's eyes. "Let go of me, Frank."

"Not until you talk to me. You've taken this too far, sweetie, and I think you know it."

Stay calm. Frank had to know he'd be even more fucked if he hurt her again. Especially with a street full of witnesses this time.

"Don't call me sweetie," she said in the coldest voice she could muster. "I broke up with you, remember?"

His condescending smile made her want to scream. "We both know you didn't mean that."

She wanted to punch him in the mouth. To claw at his eyes. To scream every enraged thought she'd ever had about him at the top of her lungs.

But Tabitha had made it abundantly clear that she couldn't give in to any of those desires. Right now, she had all the power. In a legal sense anyway. The dumbest thing she could possibly do would be to give it up.

With a calmness she didn't remotely feel, she gave the hand gripping her upper arm a pointed look, and then glanced at the credit union across the street. "That bank's security cameras are recording us right now. And as I understand it, it was a condition of your bail that you're not allowed to contact me in any way. So I'm going to say it one more time, Frank. Let go of me."

The smug confidence drained from his eyes more and more with each word. By the time she finished speaking, it had been replaced by something else—something she'd never seen in all her years with him.

Fear.

A feeling of power crackled and buzzed inside her with all the intensity of an imminent thunderstorm. When Frank pulled his hand away and took a step back, it was like lightning striking her heart, charging her, bringing her back to life.

"Don't contact me again," she said, striding past him and straight into the Fairford Inn, never once looking back.

CHAPTER 7

Jonathan

Thank fuck for Eve.

It wasn't the first time the thought crossed Jonathan's mind. Hell, it probably wasn't even the hundredth. Everything on the expansion project had turned around, all thanks to her.

True to her word, Eve emailed him with two potential construction companies the morning after the failed consultations with LGF Construction and Faber & Crane. Not only that, but each recommendation also included several paragraphs of information about the owners, the crews, and why she thought they'd do an excellent job.

The month since they hired Cox Construction flew by so fast, he had no idea where the time had gone. He supposed that's what happened when people did their jobs properly, and he didn't have to put out fires every three seconds. Lanie Cox, third generation owner of her family's company, led her team with a precision and skill that impressed him day after day.

Best of all, when it became apparent Eve knew the project inside and out, Lanie offered her a temporary contract. He had several more months of seeing her almost every day before the building would be finished.

A knock he recognized sounded on his office door—four quick beats that made his pulse speed up. Jonathan hurriedly straightened his suit, even though he knew it looked perfect already, then called out, "Come in."

Eve pushed open the door, and the sight of her took his breath away for a moment. "Oh, wow." He didn't mean to speak the words aloud and was damn glad he'd never been prone to blushing. At her surprised expression, he hurried to add, "I love what you've done with your hair."

Her smile lit up the entire room like a beacon, drawing him to her. "Really?" she asked, reaching up to pat a gentle hand over the newly styled locks. "It's not too much?"

Too much? Christ, it was fucking perfect. Over the weekend, she'd had striking red highlights added to her dark, coffee brown hair. Her usual ponytail nowhere to be seen, her hair tumbled over her shoulders in beautiful waves, coming to a stop over her breasts.

Do. Not. Stare. At. Her. Breasts.

Fuck, this was getting harder and harder every day. Because it wasn't just the hair—not by a long shot. It was all of her.

Gone were the mom jeans and shapeless old DHFT Construction T-shirts covered in stains. Though she still looked ready to get to work on the new building in her steel-toed work boots, the jeans were much more formfitting. The shirt looked like it was actually made for a woman, accentuating her delicious curves rather than hiding them.

But he couldn't say any of that. He'd spent the last month doing everything he could to *not* obsess over those perfect lips, or stare at the sway of her ass when she walked away from him.

Eve coughed politely, and he realized he'd been silent for way too long. Shit, what had she asked? Oh right—if her new hairstyle was too much.

"Not even remotely," he said, needing to clear his throat and try again before the words would come out. "The red really suits you."

That was the understatement of the century. She looked like a siren, beckoning him to abandon his course and aim forevermore in her direction.

If he wasn't careful, he'd be dashed upon the rocks any second now.

She patted the side of her hair again, like she wasn't used to the feel of it down yet. "I used to dye my hair all the time when I was younger, but Frank thinks women with unnatural hair colors are trashy. So I wanted to do something drastic, cause fuck him." She laughed nervously. "That's probably a stupid reason to do something, isn't it?"

"No, don't start doing that," Jonathan said, voice kind but firm.

Frowning, she asked, "Doing what?"

"Looking to other people for approval. Talley manipulated you into seeking his approval for everything you did, didn't he?"

Her frown deepened as she considered his words. After several tense seconds, she nodded.

"Fuck that," he said, startling a small laugh out of her. "You don't need anyone's approval but your own. Did you want to dye your hair?"

"Yes," she said, smiling.

"Then that's all that matters. Who gives a fuck what your reason was so long as you're happy." He found himself mirroring her expression without even meaning to. He hadn't smiled this much in months, not since he visited home for Christmas.

He'd always been far too serious for his own good, even as a child—something his two younger sisters never missed a chance to remind him of. His family always managed to bring out his lighter side eventually, but few others ever discovered that power. It served him well as a CEO, when he, Mason, and Leo founded HSS Biotech right out of college. His demeanor made him seem older and helped people take him seriously.

Though he supposed his wealth had just as much to do with it, if not more. Jonathan and Leo both came from money and had no problem throwing around their trust funds to get their foot in several important doors. Mason found the whole thing obscene from the start, and Jonathan cringed now at some of the shit he and Leo pulled.

Hard to argue with results, though. By the time they sold the company seven years later, determined to open Fairford Manor instead, they had over five hundred employees.

The three of them never needed to worry about money again.

Eve slid a manila folder across his desk, drawing his mind back to the present. "Purchase orders for your approval," she said, face still aglow with pleasure at his words. "Shoot me a text when you've had a chance to go through them, and I'll pick them up."

Resting his hands on top of the folder, he smiled at her. "I can bring them to you for once. I assure you I'm capable of walking down two flights of stairs."

She chuckled. "Just trying to make your life easier. Lainey and I are determined to make this experience the complete opposite of what happened with Frank."

"I appreciate that." And he really did, more than he knew how to say. Things improved so much in the last month that he finally had time to start seeing guests again. Thank God for that, because he needed to burn off this energy humming just beneath his skin before he did something monumentally stupid.

Like bend Eve over his desk and fuck her once and for all.

Distraction time. "I talked to Lainey this morning, actually," he said, leaning back in his chair and stretching out his long legs. "She couldn't be happier with how easy you've made this transition for her crew. There's potential for you there, I think."

Her answering grin sent a wave of warmth washing over him. "She's hinted a couple times now that she might want to hire me permanently. I can't even believe it. I'd *love* to work for Lainey. She's such a badass."

"I find it very easy to believe," he said, reveling in the joy written in every inch of her body. It felt like he'd been half empty all his life, never even realizing it. These little moments with her filled him up a little bit at a time. If this kept up, he'd be full near to bursting before long.

She planted her hands on her hips. "Flattery won't get you anywhere," she teased. "You still have to sign the POs."

"It's not flattery if it's true," he shot back, enjoying the flash of pleasure in her dark eyes. "You're just as much of a badass as Lainey. Of course she wants you on her team."

Eve's lower lip trembled, and for a moment he thought she would start crying. But then she gave the stack of Manor applications on one corner of his desk a pointed look, her whole demeanor shifting like she'd just donned a mask. "And how are things going for you professionally?" A soft, rosy color tinted her cheeks. "Any good contenders lately?"

Jonathan lifted a single eyebrow. "Contenders?" he repeated, one corner of his mouth lifting. "Are we fucking or boxing?"

She rolled her eyes. "You know what I mean. I haven't seen you with any guests for a while, but it looks like that's about to change?"

Would it bother you to see me with another woman instead of you? The question almost tumbled out of his mouth, but he thought better of it at the last second. He needed to keep this professional. Picking up the topmost application, he pretended to peruse the first page. "Now that the crisis is over, I need to get back to work," he said as nonchalantly as he could.

Leaning on the edge of his desk, she plucked the application from his hand. "Miranda Kushner," she said, eyes moving back and forth as she read the page. "Thirty-one years old. Just ended a ten-year relationship with her Dom and is looking for something commitment free to fill her lonely days. My, my." She met his gaze and arched her dark brows. "I thought you didn't like being a rebound."

A warning alarm started blaring and flashing red in his brain. "I don't think that's quite what I said," he answered carefully, not liking the shrewd look in her eyes. "And you really shouldn't be looking at the applications, at least not without signing an NDA first."

"Close enough." She ignored him when he held out a hand, her gaze returning to the application. "And I did sign an NDA," she reminded him, flipping through several of the pages without even glancing at them. "I can't talk about anything I see on Manor property while employed here. Ahh, here we are. Let's see what Miranda's into."

She'd gone straight to the first page of hard and soft limits, as if she knew exactly where to find it. He filed that bit of information away for later.

"Hmm," Eve said, moving onto the second page of limits, then quickly to the third. "Not a lot of fives on here. What a shame."

The application had seven full pages of potential sexual activities a guest could engage in with her Dom. Each option got a rating between one and five, giving the Manor's five Doms insight into whether their kinks were compatible or not. The stack of applications on his desk were all from women who, at a quick glance at least, seemed like a good fit for Jonathan's current mood.

"Honestly, this one seems almost vanilla," she said with a little tsking noise. "Given what I've seen go on around here, I don't think this is the place for her."

"Give it back, Eve," Jonathan said, losing patience with her little act. He held out a hand again. "Now."

Not even acknowledging that he spoke, she reached for the second application on the stack. Oh, how he wanted to spank her.

This time he caught her wrist in his hand. "Enough. Why are you acting like this?"

Eve went perfectly still, staring at where his fingers wrapped around her wrist for several seconds, eyes big and round. Her breath came in short, quick bursts.

"Look at me, please," he said, soft and low this time.

It took several seconds for her to comply. Her eyes looked panicked, almost wild.

"I'm not going to hurt you," he told her, loosening his grip but not letting go. "You're safe with me. You'll *always* be safe with me. I give you my word."

The wild look in her eyes melted away, giving way to embarrassment. "I'm sorry," she whispered, dropping Miranda's application on the desk between them. "I don't know what came over me."

He held onto her for a little longer, marveling in how small her wrist felt in his hand. Her work had made her strong, but no amount of heavy lifting could change how petite her bone structure was. "Your fear is perfectly understandable," he said in that same, calming voice. "If you'll allow it, I'd like to help you. I know how much you want to be in the lifestyle."

Eve gulped and looked down at her wrist again. "Yes, please," she managed in a hoarse whisper.

"But first, I want to know what was going on before I grabbed you. Tell me why you acted like that."

When at last he let go, she rocketed off the desk and across the room. "I'm sorry," she muttered again, wrenching the door open. "I need to get back to work." A moment later, she disappeared from view, leaving nothing but unanswered questions in her wake.

Jonathan couldn't focus worth a fuck, and he knew it wouldn't change until he talked to Eve again. Signing the stupid purchase orders without even looking at them, he grabbed the folder and headed downstairs.

It was a few minutes after five, so hopefully she hadn't already packed it up for the day. The crew usually worked from seven in the morning until four in the afternoon, relying on the Manor's excellent sound-proofing to keep the noise from disturbing guests. But Eve frequently stuck around longer, leaving an hour or two after Lainey and the others.

Questions swirled through his mind as he raced down the first set of stairs and along the second-floor hallway. Had she been looking at the Manor's application? Is that how she knew exactly which page to flip to?

And her bratty comments about that other woman's application— what the fuck was that about? Disdain for his job?

No, that couldn't be it. He'd known her more than seven months now, and the only reaction she'd ever had to his job was lust.

Jealousy then? Admittedly, the thought pleased him a little bit. He'd started to worry that as more time passed since her split with Talley, her interest would start to wane. Before today, she'd been perfectly profes-sional in all of their interactions.

Please let it be jealousy.

As he reached the bottom of the grand staircase, Zach waved him over to the reception desk. The younger man wore his customary vest and bow tie, the latter the same bright green as his eyes. He'd been favoring that one a lot recently; his fiancé, Remy, gave it to him for Christmas, and Zach had always been a hopeless romantic.

"I hear you've been rummaging around in the application room," Zach said, smirking as Jonathan crossed the lobby's gleaming marble tiles. "You ready to dive back into the fray?"

Jonathan pursed his lips, trying not to smile. "It hasn't been that long since I had a guest, has it?"

Eyes twinkling with amusement, Zach began clicking away at his laptop. "I'd have to check the reservation calendar for that. My memory doesn't go back that far."

Unable to stop it this time, Jonathan smiled. "Okay, okay. You've made your point. Consider my break officially over."

"Glad to hear it, boss." Zach's grin was more than a little smug. "Let me know when you pick one, and I'll send the letter right out." The man handwrote each and every acceptance letter on ridiculously expensive, custom-made stationary, using an antique fountain pen for his perfect calligraphy. It all seemed a bit over the top when Zach first started working at the Manor, but the guests seemed to love it.

Over the years, he'd learned to trust Zach's judgement and just roll with it.

"Will do." Maybe he'd be able to focus on the applications after he cleared the air with Eve. He'd spent a solid hour going through them early this afternoon, without retaining a single word. "Do you know if Eve left yet?"

Zach chuckled. "You're the second person to ask me that tonight. Pretty sure she's still out back."

Brows pulling together, Jonanthan asked, "Who else was looking for her?" Aiden was on vacation in Bali with his wife, Olivia, for the next two weeks. No one else in the Manor had any regular involvement with Eve or the project.

"Camden."

And least of all Camden. The man almost never took any time off, moving from guest to guest with a carefree, fuckboy glee Jonathan had never experienced, even in his long-ago frat days. He'd agreed to fund his share of the expansion so long as it didn't interrupt his schedule or disturb his guests, and he hadn't shown the remotest interest since.

"Hey, you okay?" Zach asked, his usual smirk replaced by a worried little frown.

No, he most certainly was not okay. Whatever Camden was up to, it couldn't be good. The guy was basically a walking hard-on.

"I'm fine," he said, stalking back across the lobby.

"So I can see," Zach muttered, sarcasm dripping from every word.

Jonathan ignored him, looping around the staircase and into the back hallway. Cutting through the currently empty dining room, he pushed through the two-way swinging door into the kitchen.

"Dinner won't be ready for another hour at least." Gabriel, the

Manor's head chef, didn't even look up from the pot he stirred. His sous chef was equally indifferent—Sienna only glanced up for a second before turning her attention back to her stand mixer.

The third chef straightened so dramatically she looked like a soldier coming to attention. Kendra had recently moved to dinner from the earlier shift, and even after five years at Fairford Manor, she got nervous when the partners entered the kitchen.

He ignored all three of them. Crossing the room without a word, he went through the back door, hurrying across the deserted patio to the garden beyond.

The new building stood along the left edge of the garden, situated midway between the main house and the pool. Lainey's crew had finished the outside façade in the last month, taking the building from an eyesore to something truly magnificent. The flawless white marble shone in the early evening sunlight.

Jonathan could see two people through one of the high, arched windows, but he was too far away to tell if it was Eve and Camden. Frustration had his hands fisting at his sides as he picked his way along the stone pathways, winding between the low hedges.

He nearly made it to the building when he heard voices he recognized coming out of one of the garden's many little alcoves.

"Are you sure?" Eve said.

"Trust me," Camden answered, and Jonathan had no trouble picturing the man's ridiculously handsome, dimpled face. Why did women always go nuts for the stupid fucking dimple? Of course Eve wouldn't be any different. "By the time I'm done working my magic, you'll never doubt me again."

Her laugh drifted out of the alcove, high and clear. No sign of the nerves she sometimes showed around him. "You're awfully cocky."

"Oh, baby, you have no idea," Camden said, oozing so much charm Jonathan knew Eve would never be able to resist. "If you don't have at least three orgasms by the time the night is up, I'll take a vow of chastity."

Every single muscle in his body tensed as Eve's laughter filled his ears again.

He'd never wanted to beat the ever-loving shit out of one of his friends before.

But there was a first time for everything.

With cold fury flowing through him like literal ice in his veins, he stormed into the alcove.

CHAPTER 8

Eve

"If you want that hand to stay attached to your body, I suggest you remove it from her thigh."

Eve shrieked in surprise, nearly falling off the white wrought iron bench when she whipped around. Jonathan was here. The plan had been in place for all of twenty seconds and he was already fucking *here*.

As for Camden, he hardly reacted at all, catching her with ease before leaning oh-so-casually against the bench's back, legs spread wide. "Jonathan," he said, his hand once again resting on her upper thigh. He grinned despite the threat of imminent bodily harm. "What a lovely surprise."

"I'm not fucking around, Camden," Jonathan practically growled, glaring at his longtime business partner and friend like a mortal enemy. "Get. Your hand. Off."

Eve's heart fluttered in her chest, even if this version of Jonathan scared her the tiniest bit. Thank God that fiery anger wasn't directed at her.

Camden only grinned wider. "I believe the lady can say for herself who can and cannot touch her." The bold son of a bitch even gave her leg a little squeeze.

The two men stared at each other for several tense seconds, the only sound the pounding of her heartbeat in her own ears. She could hardly fucking breathe.

Eve screamed again when Jonathan lurched forward, grabbing two fistfuls of Camden's tight black T-shirt. Though the men were of a similar height, Camden easily had fifty pounds on Jonathan, all of it muscle. It wouldn't be a contest if it came down to a fistfight.

The disparity didn't even seem to cross Jonathan's mind. He hauled the larger man off the bench as if he weighed nothing, dragging him several feet away. The sound of fabric tearing filled the air as Camden's shirt ripped at the shoulder seams.

Oh fuck, oh fuck. Eve had no idea what to do. Camden told her to let whatever happened play out—that he could handle himself. But Jonathan looked ready to quite literally rip the man's head off.

Enough. She had to stop this before things got out of hand. She opened her mouth to tell Jonathan the truth, but never got the chance.

"Eve is *mine.*" Jonathan was right up in Camden's face, their noses nearly touching. "If you ever lay your hand on what's mine again, I'll fucking kill you. Do you understand me?"

Her heart beat so fast, she feared she might have a goddamn heart attack.

Mine.

That word reverberated in her head like the ring of a cathedral bell, clear and beautiful and endless.

Camden turned his head, throwing her a smug glance. "See? I told you it would work."

The rage flickered in Jonathan's dark eyes before going out completely. "Excuse me?" After a few seconds, he let go of Camden's ruined shirt, backing up a step.

"She—" Camden started.

"Shut up," Jonathan ordered, holding up a hand to stop him. He turned to face her, where she still sat huddled on the bench. "I want to hear this from you."

She suddenly felt like a naughty student sent to the principal's office. Unable to stop herself from squirming, she fixed her gaze on the severe line of his lips as she answered in a small voice. "I sent in an application last week."

Those furious lips parted as he drew in a sharp breath. "Why the hell did you do that?"

"Because I couldn't think of any other way to get your attention," she admitted, mortification making every inch of her skin burn. "But you didn't even notice."

She risked a glance up at his eyes. The anger had disappeared, but she couldn't read the new expression there.

"Zach told her you only took applications from the *Fifty Shades Lite* pile," Camden said, smirking. "You know—the pile he normally has to force us to go through so he can send out the rejection letters. What's that about?"

Jonathan kept his gaze locked with hers while he snarled, "I said shut up, and I fucking meant it."

Clearly not remotely intimidated, Camden laughed. "It's not her fault you're oblivious. Can you blame the woman for taking matters into her own hands?"

Ignoring the other man completely, Jonathan continued to stare her down with that peculiar look in his eyes. "This was a set-up."

It was a statement, not a question. Still, she felt compelled to respond. "Zach helped me come up with a plan. And Camden—"

"I overheard their scheming and volunteered my services," he interrupted proudly. "I'm all for delayed gratification, but this is extreme, brother."

"Fuck you," Jonathan said, giving Camden a hard look. "You've never delayed your gratification once in your life."

Camden grinned in response. "You wound me. Now, if you'll excuse me, I need to get back to my guest. I'm sure you two have a lot to talk about. Also, you owe me a new shirt." He sauntered out of the alcove and toward the main house as if he hadn't a care in the world.

God, she envied his confidence. She'd never felt that sure of herself for even one second in her entire life.

Least of all right now. Something very close to panic coursed through her as she tried—and failed—to make herself meet Jonathan's eyes again.

The silence between them dragged out, making her even more

nervous. She'd give anything to know what he was thinking right now but was far too terrified to ask.

At long last, he stepped slowly toward her, coming to a stop right at the edge of the bench, one of his legs nestled between her thighs, forcing them to spread. "Look at me," he said, cupping her chin in his hand.

She didn't resist as he tilted her head back, finally daring to look into his eyes. Anger still lingered there, making her wince. But something far more powerful waited beneath it—a lust that made her blood feel like liquid fire in her veins.

Mine. She remembered the way he'd said the word, like he would fight whoever dared challenge his claim.

Like he was sure he would win.

"Jonathan—" she started.

"You will refer to me as Sir during our scenes. Do you understand?"

Holy fuck. She needed a new pair of panties.

"Yes, Sir."

"Good girl. Now answer these questions for me as honestly and succinctly as possible. If someone other than me had seen your application and approached you, what would you have done?"

"Told them the truth," she answered simply. "I only want you."

The lust flared in his eyes, overpowering the anger. "Do you know where your application is right now?"

"Zach has it."

"What did you choose as your safeword?"

She held up her hand, wiggling her finger until the square-cut gem caught a beam of sunlight. "Emerald."

"You're not officially a guest at this resort. So I need you to grant your permission to do whatever I please to you for the rest of the night unless you use your safeword."

Eve squirmed on the hard bench. She'd need new jeans, too. "Yes, Sir, you have my permission."

Letting go of her chin, Jonathan took her hands in his, pulling her to her feet. The hardness in his eyes softened as he looked down at her. "You can use your safeword for anything when you're with me." A new kind of urgency had entered his voice. "If you want to stop for literally any reason, no matter how big or small, you have the right to stop.

Always. I won't be mad. I won't give you the silent treatment. I'll never treat your decision to end a scene with anything other than respect. Do you understand?"

At some point as he spoke, she'd stopped breathing. She didn't even remember doing it. Drawing air into her lungs, she tried desperately not to cry. *You're fucking perfect.* Refusing to let those words pass her lips, she instead said, "Yes, Sir, I understand."

"Good girl. Follow me." With that, he turned and moved out of the alcove with long, swift strides, and she had to run to catch up. Even once she walked right behind him, her much shorter legs required two steps for every one of his.

He led them on the quickest path to the main patio doors, hardly even slowing as he pulled open one of the French doors and continued inside. Eve carefully shut the door behind her, not wanting to damage the glass, then scurried to catch up again.

When they emerged from the back hallway, Jonathan finally stopped, turning to face her at the base of the stairs. "Stay here," he ordered, then crossed the lobby to the reception desk. He held out his hand without a word.

Eyes shining with amusement, Zach pulled her application out of a desk drawer and handed it over. "Enjoy," he said, his usual half-smile becoming a straight-up grin.

With a low, furious huff, Jonathan turned and strode back to her, each step on the marble tiles echoing in the high-ceilinged room. Taking hold of her hand, he led her around the staircase and down the hallway, past multiple rooms she'd never entered. The dining room, billiard room, and formal parlor flashed by so fast, she hardly got to look at them. Only the study and bathroom were familiar to her.

When at last he stopped, they stood before the final door in the corridor—the only one with a keypad above the handle. Jonathan hit six numbers so fast, she only caught the first two. When he hit the large lock symbol at the bottom, the door unlocked with a soft clicking sound.

As soon as he pulled the door open, a low, sensuous beat drifted up the stairs from below, loud enough to vibrate in her chest. Man, this place didn't fuck around when it came to their soundproofing. No wonder the guests never complained about early morning construction noise.

Still grasping her hand, Jonathan led her slowly down the stairs, careful not to tug her forward and make her fall.

"Oh my God," Eve gasped when they reached the room below. Her eyes widened until they couldn't go any farther.

"Have you ever been in a dungeon before?"

She raked her gaze over the enormous, gray-walled room. She had no clue what most of the stuff in here was even called, but she had no trouble figuring out the purpose of it all.

Pleasure and pain. In a place like this, the two would be so deeply intertwined that it would be impossible to tell where one ended and the other began.

It took her several seconds to find her voice. "No, Sir."

"Are you afraid?"

Her gaze snapped up to meet his. She stood a little taller. "No, Sir."

His lips spread into a slow smile that set a whole slew of butterflies fluttering in her stomach. He was, without a doubt, the most beautiful man she'd ever seen. With that ridiculous jawline, the hair so perfectly styled she felt sure she'd never be brave enough to touch it, and by God those cheekbones . . . the man belonged on billboards or movie screens, not here.

Definitely not with her, of all people.

Not that Eve thought she wasn't pretty. She'd never had any trouble attracting the opposite sex. In fact, Frank used to get so jealous of the way the crew looked at her that he forced her to wear all those baggy clothes on jobsites. But she was still a sort-of-unemployed construction worker. And the man standing before her was like a literal god.

"What are you thinking?" Jonathan asked, cupping her face between both hands.

"That you're way out of my league," she admitted.

He laughed, the sound low and rich and delicious. "Quite the opposite, I think." Eve wanted to argue, but he didn't give her the chance. "Raise your arms above your head."

Her pussy clenched as she followed his instructions.

"Good girl. Now don't move." Letting her application drop to the floor, he pulled her T-shirt up, lifting it free of her arms before dropping it next to the packet of paper. Approval filled his eyes as he ran a single finger down the satin strap of her bra, then across the top edge of the crimson lace. "So sexy," he murmured, brushing the pad of his thumb over her nipple until it hardened. "Not at all what I expected to find."

In truth, her usual undergarments were a hell of a lot more practical. No point in getting all dressed up just to get sweaty and filthy at work. But ever since she mailed in her application, she'd chosen one of her sexier lingerie sets each morning. She even tried her hardest not to be so hands on with the build, just in case.

She was grateful for that foresight now that she stood half-naked before him.

"I wore it for you," she said, drawing in a sharp breath when he rolled her nipple between two fingers. "I'm glad you like it."

Humming appreciatively, he slid his hand down her bare belly, making her shiver as goosebumps erupted across her skin. He didn't stop when he reached the waistband of her jeans, moving lower, dropping to his knees in a single, lithe movement. His hands went to her left work boot, tugging at the laces.

"Oh shit, please don't," she said, blushing furiously, wishing she had the nerve to back away.

His hands halted, and he looked up at her with a small frown. "What's wrong?"

"Can I take my shoes and socks off myself, please?" A moment later, she added, "Sir?"

Frown deepening slightly, he asked, "Why?"

"These boots are almost a year old," she said, hoping he'd get the hint.

No dice. His brows pulled together in confusion.

"I work in them at least five days a week. Getting all dirty and sweaty and stuff." If she blushed any hotter, she'd be able to fry an egg on her forehead.

At least he didn't need her to explain any further. "Do you really think I'd care about that?" he said, censure in his voice.

In fact, she couldn't think of anything that would ruin the scene faster than him getting a whiff of that. But she couldn't bring herself to admit it out loud. "It's not exactly sexy," she said instead.

"You're wrong." He looked up so she could see the truth in his eyes. "Do you have any idea how sexy you are when you're out there working?"

Eve snorted. She couldn't help herself. "Oh, I'm sure."

He snaked a hand around her hip, giving her ass a single firm smack. Even through her Levis, it hurt. "Watch the tone," he admonished, before he got back to work on her shoelace.

Removing the boot with as much care as the prince gave to Cinderella's glass slipper, he peeled her sock off and tossed it aside. Mere moments later, he did the same on the other foot.

"Now," he said, hands running up the outsides of her legs. They drifted inward at her waist, moving to the button of her jeans. "To respond to your sarcastic comment." He slipped the button through the hole, then lowered the zipper so slowly that she almost grabbed his hand and forced him to go faster. "You're extremely smart and skilled. Everyone around you looks to you as the top expert in virtually every situation. You practically fucking glow with confidence when you're working. Why wouldn't I find that sexy?"

Eve's heart melted more with each word. Could he possibly mean it? Frank had certainly used her skills and expertise to his advantage, but he never once acted turned on by it. Quite the opposite, in fact. After a long day at work, he'd complain the whole way home about how dirty and smelly she was, insisting that she get right in the shower the moment they arrived.

When Jonathan's fingers dipped below her waistband, pushing her jeans over her hips and down her legs, her ex flew from her thoughts. His short fingernails scraped ever so lightly against her skin as he lowered the denim, making her shiver with delight.

Any second now, she'd finally be fucking Jonathan Hale. After so many months of wanting him, if he dragged this out much longer, she'd explode.

Jonathan helped her step out of her jeans, shoving them aside with the rest of her clothes. Then he leaned back on his heels, looking her up and down.

She preened a little bit, her back arching, breasts jutting out. She couldn't help it. This was her favorite bra and panty set, all skimpy satin strings and lace in the sexiest red imaginable. It made her feel a little bit wicked—a feeling she didn't often get to enjoy.

"You look good enough to eat," he said, lust making his voice raspier than normal. Leaning forward, he grabbed her hips with both hands, his fingertips digging painfully into the flesh of her ass. Before she knew what he was doing, he'd pressed his face against the front of her panties, breathing deeply.

"Oh my God," she gasped out, her legs shaky. Without thinking, she buried her hands in his perfect hair, holding onto him for dear life as his tongue darted out, pushing her panties against her clit. Her breaths came faster and faster as he continued teasing the tiny bundle of nerves, the rough scrape of lace feeling like fucking heaven.

Just when she thought for sure she'd come, he pulled away, looking up at her with smug satisfaction in his eyes. "Are you ready for your punishment?"

She squeaked in surprise, her hands dropping to her sides. "You're punishing me?" It came out rushed and breathless. Every muscle in her body screamed for the release he denied her, while her mind raced with new fears. Was he angry at her? Would this hurt?

Not the good hurt, like what she saw out by the pool. The *Frank* kind of hurt.

Standing, Jonathan cupped her face between his hands, waiting until she met his gaze to speak. "Remember that you have your safe-word. Nothing is going to happen without your consent." He brushed his thumbs along her cheekbones, the touch featherlight. "And a punishment from me isn't what you're thinking right now. I want to make you feel good, Eve. Better than you've ever felt in your life."

With a few slow breaths, she forced her racing thoughts and pounding heart to calm. This wasn't Frank. She could trust him.

Standing as tall as she could, she gave him a sweet, angelic smile. "Wouldn't you rather skip right to the fun part?" she asked, figuring it was worth a shot. "I'm not even sure I've earned a punishment."

"You most certainly have," he said with a low chuckle. "And you're not the only one." Jonathan pulled his cell out of his pocket, tapping away at the screen for several seconds. Once he finished, he turned the phone around for her to see.

The text conversation had the name Remy Levene at the top. The small, circular picture showed the Manor's event planner with his arms wrapped around Zach.

Today 5:14 PM

Your fiancé deserves one hell of a punishment for the shit he pulled today

FFS. What did he do now?

Ask him what I'm pissed about

I'm sure the fucker will be happy to tell you all about it

This should be good

"How else was I supposed to make this happen?" she said, hearing more than a little whine in her voice. She didn't want a punishment right now —even the kind he just described. She wanted him to finish what he started before she came apart at the seams.

"Oh, I don't know." He pocketed the phone, then retrieved her application from the floor. Taking her hand in his, he led her deeper into the dungeon. "You could have—and I'm just spitballing here—talked to me about it."

Eve huffed out an annoyed breath. "Okay, fair, but every time I tried you changed the subject."

"Probably should've tried harder, then," he said, stopping in front of something that looked almost like a massage table, with the face rest for her head if she were to lie on it facedown. The "table" part was shorter and narrower than a real massage table, though, and four smaller padded platforms protruded halfway down the metal legs.

Placing her application on top of a nearby cabinet full of supplies, Jonathan watched her and waited. Gratitude flowed through her that he would let the scene move at her pace.

It took a solid ten seconds longer than it should have for her to figure out what this was. "Oh," she said, unable to think of anything else to say. Though her body still longed for release, a new heat spread from her core when she pictured herself strapped to this contraption, her ass sticking out and awaiting punishment.

"Your pupils just dilated. You want me to bend you over this spanking bench, don't you?" His low voice rolled over her like distant thunder, making the hair on her arms stand on end. "You want to know what it feels like to submit to me."

"Yes, Sir, I do," she said, practically panting with need.

Without another word, he guided her into place, her torso stretched across the main padded platform and her face gently cradled in the soft, cushioned face rest. He arranged her arms and legs on the four lower platforms, securing her in place with multiple nylon straps. He cinched the straps so tight, she couldn't move at all.

Her heart pounded away like the rapid-fire beat of a snare drum. Eve always knew she was different. That she longed for things most other people didn't—things she didn't even fully know how to define herself. All she knew was that without at least some pain, she couldn't lose herself in pleasure. Her body would remain unsatisfied, demanding more.

She thought she found what she needed in her last relationship, at least at first. But now she knew how profoundly wrong she'd been.

Eve had never felt like this before. Never felt like every nerve in her body was on high alert, soaking in more sensation than she ever knew possible.

Looping two fingers beneath the satin strings of her panties, Jonathan pulled them down with agonizing slowness, forcing her to feel just how wet they were as they slid down her legs. He left the scraps of satin and lace there around her knees, and she had no idea why that turned her on so much.

"I'm gonna die," she said, not sure if she was complaining or thanking him.

"Only if you're very lucky," he answered. Seconds later, the sound of rustling paper reached her ears.

The application. He was finally taking a proper look at her hard and soft limits.

Please don't be disappointed.

"Oh, Eve," he said after a full two minutes. "You and I are going to be fucking perfect together."

When Jonathan brought the end of a riding crop down on her ass a second later, she burst into tears. Not because it hurt too much. But because it hurt more perfectly than anything she'd ever felt in her life.

"Do you want to use your safeword?" he asked, concern filling his voice.

"Oh God, I'll die if you stop now," she forced out through her tears. "Please give me more. *Please.*"

"That's my girl," Jonathan said, striking twice more, one right after the other. "Let yourself feel it. This is what your body needs."

Closing her eyes, she focused on the sensations coursing through her as the crop continued to fall. Eve pulled against the straps, needing to feel them bite into her skin.

She didn't just want to know that she couldn't escape. She wanted to feel it.

Once every inch of her ass was on fire, Jonathan moved down to her thighs, the new pain taking her breath away. Jesus fuck, it hurt *so good.*

A flurry of sharp slaps to her sit spots made her scream, though she didn't remember deciding to do so. "Please!" Her sobs drew the word out into several syllables. "I need you. I need you so much."

The riding crop hit the floor with a loud clatter. Seconds later, she felt the thick head of his cock press against her entrance.

His hands grasped her hips, his fingers pressing against her pelvic bone enough to hurt. "You're mine." It was a declaration. A claiming. A promise.

Then he rammed his hips forward, pushing into her so deep and so fast that she screamed again, certain she'd just been split in two. Rocking back, he slid most of the way out of her, then pushed forward again, no gentler than the first stroke. This time, though, her pussy accepted him gratefully, even greedily. She clenched her internal muscles, never wanting to feel empty again.

Little good did it to her. Jonathan started up a steady rhythm after that, pumping in and out of her, slamming the tops of her thighs against the edge of the main platform with bruising force. He hadn't even undressed before taking her. The teeth of his zipper dug into her punished bottom with each thrust, making her hiss at the exquisite pain.

So good. So fucking good. Pleasure built up inside her like a colossal wave, rolling higher and higher. She didn't know how much more she could take before it all came crashing down.

"Come for me, Eve," Jonathan said, tilting his hips, pushing into her at a slightly different angle.

That was all it took. Her orgasm exploded from her center, pulsing through her, making every muscle in her body seize. Jonathan followed her moments later, his scream blending with hers, together rising above the constant beat of the music.

When at last the final aftershocks subsided, Eve sagged against the spanking bench, her arms and legs feeling almost numb, her skin tingly and damp with sweat.

Not once, for even a moment, had she imagined sex could feel this fucking good. "Please, Sir," she panted, still trying to catch her breath. "Please tell me we don't have to wait long before we can do that again."

CHAPTER 9

Jonathan

Checking her phone for the thousandth time, Eve sighed and continued fidgeting in the passenger seat of his car. She seemed to worry she might not feel it vibrate, even with her fingers wrapped tightly around it.

"Give it to me," Jonathan said, his tone brooking no argument.

Sighing, she placed her phone in his outstretched hand. "I'm sorry. I'm just nervous."

He dropped the phone into one of the cupholders, then placed a hand on her thigh, moving his thumb back and forth in a soothing motion. "You have nothing to worry about. I told you, Lainey approved the time off. She assured me she has no problem with it."

Her exact words had actually been, *"Oh, thank God. If you two didn't start fucking soon, I was going to 'accidentally' lock you in a dark room and lose the key. Go get this out of your systems before we all go crazy."* Apparently the "lovesick puppy looks" they directed at each other were a great subject of gossip among the new crew.

Jonathan had no idea what she was talking about. He'd never been lovesick in his entire life. But he wasn't about to argue since it got him exactly what he wanted.

When he'd met Eve in the Manor's parking lot that morning, guiding her into his car and driving away without explanation, she practically begged him to turn around, not wanting to be late for work. Even after all his assurances, she still expected an angry text or call from her boss any second.

"Do you trust me?" he asked when he saw her eyeing the phone, hardly even blinking.

After a few seconds, she let out a long sigh and finally relaxed into the seat. "Yes. I do."

"Then please believe me that everything will be one hundred percent fine, and just try to enjoy this, okay?" He said it gently, not wanting her to think she'd upset him, too.

"Okay," she agreed. "Sorry I'm so tense. Spontaneity isn't really my strong suit."

To be honest, it wasn't his, either. But as he lay in bed last night, the smell of her still on him, too intoxicating for sleep to be possible, an idea popped into his head. Once the seed was planted, he couldn't stop thinking about it until he put things in motion.

"I thought you were taking a new client?" Zach had teased when Jonathan told him about his plans first thing this morning.

"Oh, fuck off." Jonathan did his best to look stern. "Don't make me tell Remy to punish you again. Your ass can't be feeling super great this morning."

Zach had thrown his head back with delighted laughter. "You can't say things like that to your employees, you know," he said, bright green eyes dancing with mirth. "I should report you to HR."

"Unfortunately for you, I'm the closest thing we have to an HR department." Jonathan hadn't been able to stop himself from smiling. "Consider your complaint noted."

Now here they were an hour and a half later, skirting around the edges of Burlington, and he still couldn't keep a smile off his face for longer than a few seconds.

"Do you think I could at least get a hint?"

In answer, Jonathan pointed at a road sign, simultaneously moving over to the exit lane.

"The *airport*?" Her voice went up a whole octave on the second word. "We're going on a trip?"

"Don't worry," he said as he exited the I-89, maneuvering the car through the tight curve of the ramp. "I'll have you back in time for work Monday morning."

"But . . ." For a few moments, she seemed at a total loss. "I don't even have a suitcase."

He smiled, taking hold of her hand and giving it a squeeze. "We'll take care of that when we get there. For now, just sit back and try to relax."

She stopped asking questions after that, instead staring through the windshield as he drove them the rest of the way to the airport. Her hands fidgeted adorably in her lap.

It wasn't until they got to the departures area that she spoke again. "Wait, aren't we supposed to go in there?" she asked, pointing at the tiny airport's only parking garage.

"Trust me," he said, stopping the car right in front of a woman wearing a well-tailored pantsuit. Her stick-straight, auburn hair was cut into a short bob. She hurried to open the passenger side door.

"Welcome to Burlington International Airport, Ms. Hutchinson," she said, grinning as a bewildered Eve climbed out of the car. As soon as Eve moved out of the way, the woman shut the door and moved around to the trunk, moving his small, black rolling suitcase to the curb. When she made it to Jonathan's side of the car, she smiled again. "I'm Angel-ica. We spoke on the phone this morning."

"Keys are in the ignition," he told her, pulling his wallet out of his pocket. "I'll text you when I know what our plans are for the return flight."

The woman gave him a thousand-megawatt smile when he handed her what looked like three or four hundred-dollar bills. "Of course, Mr. Hale. I'll make sure I'm waiting at arrivals when you and Ms. Hutchinson get back."

"I appreciate it, Angelica."

With a final grin, she slipped behind the wheel, quickly adjusted the seat and rearview mirror, and closed the door. Seconds later, his Astin Martin pulled out into the minimal departures traffic, looping around the road and out of sight.

"Um, what just happened?" Eve muttered as he joined her on the sidewalk.

Jonathan frowned. "What's wrong?"

"The parking garage is literally right there." She pointed at the four-story building across the street.

Understanding washed over him, and for a moment he felt mildly embarrassed. Rubbing the back of his neck, he made himself admit, "I don't really like parking garages. I came home from a business trip several years ago and someone had fucked up the entire driver's side of my car. Bastard didn't even leave a note." Probably realized they'd just mangled a Porsche and hauled ass out of there. He supposed he couldn't blame them.

"So where is she taking your car?" Eve asked, looking over her shoulder as he led her into the airport terminal.

"To a small, private garage nearby," he answered, leaving out exactly how private of a garage it was. In truth, a friend who lived forty-five minutes away let Jonathan use one of the five garage bays at his home. Whenever he flew out of Burlington, he paid one of the local limo companies cash to loan him one of their drivers to ferry the car back and forth.

It had always seemed a perfectly reasonable solution to his problem before. Now, seeing it through Eve's eyes, he wondered if maybe he was being a tad ridiculous.

Luckily, she let the matter drop, eyeing his suitcase now instead. "How come you get a bag?" she complained. "You get to change your clothes, and I have to be grungy all weekend?"

He gave her a mischievous grin. "Who said I have clothes in here?"

Her eyes got so wide, he could see the whites all the way around her irises. She swallowed nervously as he led her into the airport and toward security, towing the suitcase behind him. "Wow, this airport's even smaller than I thought," she said, eyeing the almost non-existent line.

"Have you never flown out of here before?" he asked while they wound between the line divider ropes. Her home with Frank hadn't been too far from Burlington.

"Flights out of Boston or Manchester are usually way cheaper," she answered, digging her wallet out of her purse and producing her driver's license. "We didn't travel much, but when we did, Frank was super particular about that."

Nothing about that surprised him in the least.

Minutes later, they were through security and walking down the terminal. "Here we go," he said, steering her to what had long since become a familiar gate. The sign behind the desk read only, *Private Flight*.

"Holy fuck," Eve muttered under her breath, eyes wide as she walked up to the bay of floor-to-ceiling windows. The private jet waiting at the end of the boarding bridge gleamed in the early morning sunlight. "This . . . this is for us?"

Moving up behind her, Jonathan rested his hands on her shoulders. "This is for you," he said softly. "Everything this weekend is for you."

She twisted around, wrapping her arms around his neck and crushing her lips against his. He grabbed hold of her, digging his fingers into the sharp jut of her shoulder blades, pressing her body flush against his as he deepened the kiss.

Christ, she felt good. Almost too good—if he let this last much longer, they wouldn't be going anywhere but a jail cell for indecent exposure.

Longing for the freedoms he enjoyed at the Manor, he forced himself to pull away. "Come on," he said, grabbing the suitcase handle and leading her toward the short, middle-aged man waiting at the podium by the boarding door. Jonathan wasn't sure where he'd come from. The gate was deserted when they arrived. "Let's get on the plane before things get too out of hand."

No one would care what they did once they reached cruising height, so long as he tipped well enough. And Jonathan Hale was nothing if not an exceptional tipper.

"You're still not going to tell me where we are? Seriously?" Eve crossed her arms over her stomach as the chartered jet taxied up to a gate.

"Aren't surprises fun?" he teased, tugging at her arms until she relented and uncrossed them. Taking both her hands in his, he brought them up to his lips, kissing the back of her left hand, then her right. "I'm taking you somewhere very special to me. Is that enough to tide you over for now?"

Heaving a dramatic sigh, she said, "Oh, I suppose so." She went back to staring out the window. That didn't stop him from seeing the tiny smile she tried to hide.

Once they made it into the airport itself, her head swiveled from side to side as she read every sign in sight, searching for clues. It was one of those little gift shops with the snacks and magazines that finally gave it away. "Denver?" she said, darting over to grab a burnt orange hoodie with the city name and an artistic rendition of the Rocky Mountains on the front. "We're in Denver?"

Giving the hoodie an appraising look, he nodded once as he made his decision. "That would look adorable on you," he said, taking it from her hand and walking over to the register.

"You don't have to buy me a sweatshirt," she said, trailing after him. He didn't have to see her face to know she'd just rolled her eyes.

"It gets cold here at night," he said, tapping his AmEx on the credit card machine. Tucking his wallet back into his pocket, he accepted the bag from the bored cashier. "Besides, you love this color."

Her lovely brows arched up in surprise. "Why do you think I love this color?"

"All the new shirts you've been wearing to work," he explained, hoping he hadn't gotten this entirely wrong. "Several of them have either burnt orange or emerald green on them. I . . ." He hesitated, not sure how to read her expression. "I assumed that meant they were your favorite colors. But if I'm wrong—"

"You're not wrong at all," she said, going up on her toes to plant a kiss on his lips. "I just didn't realize you were paying that much attention."

Reaching up with his free hand, he brushed her beautiful, red-streaked hair away from her face. "I always pay attention to you."

If she were an anime character, there would be little hearts in her eyes right now. It was fucking adorable.

"Come on," he said, taking her hand and leading her away from the little newsstand. He gripped the bag and suitcase handle in his other hand, the bottom of the plastic bag resting against the top of his luggage. "I have a car waiting."

"Of course you do." She shook her head. "Wait, if we were only flying to Denver, why did you book a private plane? Every airline in America probably flies here."

With a little shrug, he admitted, "We'd have to drive all the way down to Boston to get a nonstop flight."

She blinked up at him for a few seconds, utter disbelief written in every line of her face. For a moment, he thought maybe he'd made an error in judgement—that all he'd accomplished was to make her consider him a rich, entitled asshole.

But then she laughed, bemusement lighting her beautiful brown eyes. "Oh, man," she said, linking her arm through his as they strolled through the airport. "Being your girlfriend is going to be a whole new experience for me, isn't it?"

Girlfriend?

They were fucking. Not dating. Hell, they only even started doing that under twenty-four hours ago.

And yet, he'd spent the last seven months of his life wanting to be near her as much as possible. In fact, he wanted to be around her so much that mere hours after they finally got involved, he surprised her with romantic weekend away. At one of the most important places to him in the world.

A place he'd never brought anyone before.

Yeah, okay, she was absolutely his girlfriend.

Holy shit. That was new.

Jonathan thought maybe he should be panicking right now, or even planning his escape route back to the plane. But none of those feelings materialized.

Instead, a warmth spread out from his chest, making him feel like he'd just stepped into a bright beam of sunshine.

Pulling his arm free of hers, he wrapped it around her shoulders, tucking her snugly against his side. "You'll get used to it."

CHAPTER 10

Eve

"That's us," Jonathan said, pointing as they walked down the wide Arrivals sidewalk. A balding man in a rumpled suit stood in front of older model Jeep Wrangler with a hideous, acid-green paint job and a black soft top. He looked supremely bored as he stared down at his phone, scrolling listlessly.

As they got closer to the older man, Eve noticed the car's license plate read SLIMER. At least the paint color made sense now. She suspected the tire cover on the back had a Ghostbusters logo on it, though she didn't get a chance to check before Jonathan helped her climb into the passenger seat.

Jonathan was one surprise after another today. She never could've imagined him in a vehicle even remotely like this, yet he looked perfectly at home as he tipped the driver and got behind the wheel.

They drove a little more than an hour before arriving at an enormous, log-cabin style home in a clearing buried deep in the woods. Sunlight glinted off the seemingly endless windows, making it impossible to see what waited inside. Multiple chimneys towered above the green metal roof.

Ignoring her questions about what this place was, Jonathan led her up onto the front porch, between the two stone columns flanking the stairs. He unlocked the door with a key from the same ring holding the Jeep's key fob, beckoning for her to follow him inside.

Eve trailed her fingertips along the front door as she crossed the threshold, tracing the intricate relief carving of an oak tree with large acorns hanging from its branches. "Okay, we're here," she said, taking in as much as she could about the house as she looked for hints. "Are you finally going to tell me where we are?"

"Look around," Jonathan said, nudging her forward with a hand on the small of her back. "See if you can figure it out."

He closed the door as she turned a slow circle in the large, three-story entryway, examining the horseshoe-shaped halls above, behind cast iron railings. Wooden staircases with matching banisters and worn, forest-green carpet runners led to the upper floors. A huge chandelier that seemed to be fashioned of deer antlers hung out over the open space.

"Are we at Gaston's secret American hunting lodge?" she joked, stepping out from under the chandelier. If that thing somehow fell, she didn't want to be impaled, thank you very much.

Jonathan snorted. "Don't worry. I don't use antlers in *all* of my decorating."

She grinned, more than a little surprised by his response. "He knows lyrics to *Beauty and the Beast* songs," she said, holding her phone up to her mouth as if it were a tape recorder. "Will I ever fully understand this strange and mysterious creature, or will he shock me to the very end?"

"Oh, I hope it's the second one," he shot back, winking. "That sounds way more interesting."

Laughing, she moved deeper into the enormous house nestled in the Rocky Mountains. At least this house fit somewhat into the image she had of him in her head, despite the antlers. Big and expensive, even if some of the rugs and furniture looked past their prime. And just as private as the Manor to boot. She had a feeling there wasn't another human around for several miles at least.

Good thing he's not a serial killer, she thought, chuckling to herself as she entered a kind of great room area. She fidgeted with her ring as she looked around, twisting it absentmindedly around her middle finger.

The largest sectional sofa she'd ever seen dominated one side of the room, facing a preposterously large TV mounted on the wall. On the other side were pool and foosball tables, a well-stocked bar with a Denver Broncos logo hanging over it, and several round high-top tables with matching stools. In the far corner, a low rectangular table sported a partially built puzzle. A shelf crammed with various other jigsaw puzzles and board games stood nearby.

Okay, maybe this house didn't quite match the version of him in her head after all. This looked like a place for a large family to congregate, not a luxurious getaway for a ridiculously rich bachelor sex god and his latest conquest.

Her gaze lingered on a short bookcase in the corner behind the sectional. She wandered over there, Jonathan trailing a few feet behind. The battered wooden bookcase had clearly been much abused, with scratches and scuffs up the sides and across the top. A sizeable chunk was missing from the edge of the second shelf, but that didn't stop it from being stuffed full of worn paperbacks with no discernable organizational system.

It wasn't the books that caught her attention though, but the two large picture frames on top of the bookcase. One was a photo of four children in front of a Christmas tree—three boys ranging in age from about four to maybe ten, and an infant with a pink bow attached to her wispy brown hair.

She picked up the second frame, examining the other photo. It showed what looked like three generations of a family on a young, blond woman's wedding day. The bride and groom beamed up at her from the center of the photo, the rest of the people arranged artfully around them.

Jonathan stood to the bride's left, next to a man who was clearly his father. Same height, same broad shoulders, same cheekbones and nose. Though their eyes were different colors, they crinkled in exactly the same way when they smiled. Despite his dad being—presumably—at least twenty years his senior, they even had the same hairline.

"This is your family's house," she said softly, continuing to stare down at the picture. Jonathan looked so young . . . maybe mid-twenties? God, that felt like a lifetime ago to her. "Is this your sister?"

"One of them," he said, peering over her shoulder at the picture. He pointed at the brunette teenager standing next to him in a rose-pink bridesmaid dress. "That's my baby sister, Maisie. She was only fifteen when Alice and Dillon got married."

"How old were you?" The urge hit her to brush her fingertip over his beautiful, smiling face in the picture, but she didn't want to smudge the glass.

"Twenty-six." Predicting her next question, he added, "Alice was twenty-four."

Wow, Maisie really was his baby sister. That was one hell of an age difference.

"You grew up near San Diego," she said, remembering a comment he made on the plane. "Not Colorado."

"We spent most of our school vacations here," he explained. "Now that we're all older, we still come here every year for Thanksgiving . . . Christmas, too, when everyone can actually make it work. It's hard sometimes, though. Everyone's always so busy, and kids make everything even more challenging." His voice had taken on a faraway, wistful tone as he studied the photo of the four children—presumably his niece and nephews.

Placing the frame carefully back on top of the bookcase, Eve turned, taking in this room again now that she had this new information. She imagined a young Jonathan and Alice chasing each other around the room, shrieking with delight while their parents tried to watch the Broncos game. Next came the teenaged Jonathan and Alice sprawled on the brown-upholstered sectional, watching TV and eating chips while a preschool-aged Maisie bugged them to play with her.

She pictured everyone in the photo gathered around the pool table, laughing and teasing each other as they made terrible shots. Last of all, Jonathan as he was now and his mother—a woman with wheat blond hair and kind brown eyes—sitting in the corner putting together a puzzle in comfortable silence.

The images flashed through her mind one after the other like a slideshow, bringing tears to her eyes. This place had obviously been filled with so much love. It made her chest ache with longing to see her own dad one more time. He would've loved it here.

"Thank you for bringing me here." Facing him, she lifted her hands to his face, loving the feel of his light stubble against her skin. "It means a lot to me that you trust me with a place that's so important to you."

He placed his hands over hers, sliding them down to his neck. Then he took her face between his hands, kissing her slowly, taking his time, as if he wanted to memorize the feel of her tongue against his.

When at last he pulled away, it took her several seconds to remember how to open her eyes. He was like a drug, fogging her brain, making her feel almost disconnected from her body.

She wanted as much of him as she could possibly get.

"Do you want to see my favorite room?"

Not trusting her tongue to form words properly, she nodded, letting him lead her toward the stairs. Up they climbed, all the way to the third floor, which only had a single door. As soon as he pushed it open, sunlight streamed through from the row of tall windows on the far wall.

"Oh, wow," she said, taking in the single room that made up this floor. "It reminds me of the study at the Manor." Floor-to-ceiling bookcases lined most walls, the wood stained a dark brown. A large antique desk and rolling chair sat in one corner. In the center of the room, a brown leather loveseat and four overstuffed armchairs had been arranged in a circle with reading lamps at the corners of the space.

The only difference was the books. At the Manor, the shelves were lined with expensive, leather-bound volumes, obviously chosen for looks more than subject matter. But this place looked to be as well stocked as any indie bookstore, with a colorful variety of paperbacks and hardcovers filling every shelf. Spines were bent and dustjackets torn. Mismatched bookmarks stuck out of several of the volumes—books someone intended to finish on a later visit but hadn't yet gotten around to.

"I had Aiden model the study on this room," Jonathan admitted. "A little piece of home, even though I was so far away."

She walked over to the wall of windows. "You're far more sentimental than I ever would've guessed," she said, smiling as she looked outside. Sunlight streamed through the rare holes in the canopy, hitting the forest floor in occasional patches. It looked like a place out of a fairy tale.

With a self-conscious chuckle, he said, "Don't be too impressed. Every single one of us has fucked our fair share of guests in that room."

Laughing, she turned to face him. "Yeah, that kind of kills the home-sweet-home vibe a little bit." Good lord, he looked delicious. Even after a day of travelling, he looked ready to walk down a runway, his suit immaculate, every strand of hair in place. She cocked her head to one side. "You in the mood to desecrate this version of the room, too?"

Heat flashed in his eyes.

Eve and Jonathan started moving at the exact same time, colliding in the center of the room, mouths crushing together, hands grasping.

Gripping her ass in both hands, Jonathan lifted her, supporting her weight as she wrapped her legs around his hips. He didn't break the kiss for even a moment as he strode over to the desk, lowering her onto the surface. A pile of books tumbled loudly onto the floor, but they both ignored it.

"I want to see you," she said, her lips brushing against his as she spoke, their breath mingling. "All of you."

She'd seen him naked once before, when she watched him with a guest out by the pool. But he hadn't been hers then. She wanted to touch him, learn every single inch of him.

When she started tugging at his tie, his hands wrapped around her wrists, stopping her. "If you want me naked," he said, a delicious edge to his voice, "you're going to have to earn it."

Digging her heels into his ass, she pushed him into her, grinding herself against the bulge of his cock. "Please, Sir?"

Jonathan drew in a sharp breath, but his eyes remained determined. Burying a hand in her hair, he pulled hard enough to make her gasp. "Naughty little girls get punished." He bent to kiss and lick his way along her arched throat. "Is that what you want?" he murmured against her skin.

"No, Sir." The words came out with an involuntary moan.

"Then be good." Releasing her, he walked around the desk, sitting in the leather rolling chair with his legs spread wide. He watched her with hooded eyes, a smile playing at his lips. "Take off your clothes for me. If you want to see all of me, I'm going to see all of you first."

The command in his tone made her empty pussy clench with need.

Breath coming a little too fast, she started to strip, gripping the hem of her emerald-green shirt and lifting it slowly up over her head.

"Mmm," Jonathan said, appreciation dripping from the sound. "I love your skin. So flawless. It makes me want to mark every inch of you."

She shuddered, not able to hold back another small moan. Bending at the waist, she arched her back while she untied her boots, the image in her head of a ballet dancer, all perfect, graceful lines. In reality, she probably looked nothing like that, but lust still filled Jonathan's gaze when she straightened.

Eve kicked her boots aside, glad she'd worn simple black socks today instead of her usual old, stained tube socks. She still couldn't believe he'd peeled those things off her feet after a full day of work. It was a miracle he didn't run from her screaming then and there.

Tossing the new socks toward the shoes, she took her time unbuttoning her jeans, letting her fingers slip below the waistband, teasing along the top of her panties.

Jonathan's hands tightened on the arms of his chair. "Did I give you permission to touch yourself?" he demanded.

"No, Sir." Her hand slid ever so slightly lower.

"Eve." It was a warning. One she had no intention of heeding. Now that she knew what a punishment from Jonathan really meant, she didn't fear him in the least.

Closing her eyes, she pushed her hand lower, brushing a single fingertip over her clit.

He made it back around the desk before she had a chance to do anything more. Wrenching her jeans down to mid-thigh, he pushed her forward until she bumped against the edge of the desk. He didn't stop for even a second, forcing her to bend at the waist until her torso and cheek pressed against the smooth wood.

"What did I say about naughty girls?" he growled, gripping the back of her panties in one hand, yanking them down to just below the curve of her ass.

"They get punished, Sir." She was so turned on, she had to gasp the words out.

Leaning over the desk, he opened the top middle drawer, pulling out a wooden ruler—the old kind made of thick, sturdy wood, metal along one edge. Her heart fluttered in her chest at the sight of it.

Without another word, he began her punishment, bringing the ruler down across the center of her ass again and again without reprieve.

Holy fucking shitballs, that hurt. She clenched her cheeks together, unable to help herself.

"Relax your ass," he barked out, his rhythm not changing in the least. "Or it'll only hurt more."

Eyes screwed together and fingers digging into the unyielding surface of the desk, she tried to do as he said. "I can't," she half groaned, half wailed. It wasn't just her ass. Every single muscle in her body was taut as a bowstring.

"Suit yourself," he said, increasing the strength of each stroke.

Tears leaked from her closed eyes at the pain. Her breath came in harsh pants.

The fall of the ruler paused. A gentle hand rubbed her ass, soothing the worst of the sting. "Remember that you have your safeword."

Gratitude erupted inside her chest, making her heart feel too big for her rib cage. "I remember, Sir. I don't want to use it."

"Good girl," he said, squeezing her punished ass, making her hiss in pain.

God, it felt way too good. She couldn't hold back a moan as he started back up with the ruler. If he didn't fuck her soon, she wouldn't be able to stop herself from begging. The words were right there on the tip of her tongue.

When he aimed lower, hitting her right in her tender sit spots, she accidentally screamed. God, how embarrassing. Someone with his level of experience would want a sub with more self-control.

But the growl that rose up out of him wasn't a sound of anger. With a rush of excitement, she realized he was also losing control. Seconds later, the ruler clattered onto the desk.

Pushing her jeans and panties down to her ankles, he grabbed her around the waist and lifted her free of the ensnaring clothing. As soon as her bare feet touched the floor again, he ordered, "Kneel."

He didn't have to tell her twice. She sank to her knees on the plush area rug, mouth already salivating as he unbuckled his belt. Leaving the ends of the supple leather belt dangling, he opened his pants and freed his cock. It jutted toward her lips, so long and thick that she almost couldn't believe the whole thing had fit inside her last night. And now he wanted to put it in her mouth.

Fuck yes.

"I'm going to come in your mouth, Eve," he told her, staring down with a feral desire radiating from his wild eyes. "I want you to taste how much you please me."

In answer, she parted her lips, spreading them wide.

"Good girl," he said, pushing into her. His thrusts were shallow at first, giving her a chance to get used to his size. She did her best to wet his thick shaft, swirling her tongue around the head each time he retreated.

Pulling his belt free with a *swish* that made her shiver, he looped it around her neck, sliding the end through the buckle. "If you want to use your safeword, tap my leg twice."

She kept her hands folded on her lap as she sucked and twisted her tongue. His answering sound of satisfaction made her heart thud with pleasure.

"You like touching yourself?" he asked, pulling just hard enough for her to really feel it press against her windpipe. "Do it now. Make yourself come with my cock down your throat."

Jesus fuck. If she got any hotter, she'd burn up, leaving nothing but ash behind.

She slid her hand from her thigh to her center, moaning around his cock as she pushed two fingers inside her pussy.

"That's it," he urged, pulling the belt a little tighter as she coated her fingers. "Now touch your clit."

At the same moment she slid her slick fingertips over the tiny bud, he surged forward, pushing the head of his cock down her throat. For a handful of seconds, she gagged at the invasion, her eyes watering. But then she managed to relax her throat around him.

"Good girl," he said again, more urgently this time. "Remember what to do if you want to stop." He pulled out slowly before pushing in a little deeper than before.

Eve blinked tears out of her eyes, concentrating on keeping her throat open for him as she made tiny circles over her clit with one finger. She kept her touch featherlight, not wanting to come too soon.

Burying one hand in her hair and holding the belt tight with the other, Jonathan settled into a steady rhythm. She tried to match his rhythm with her hand, but she couldn't focus. Too many things bombarded her senses, flooding her mind, overwhelming her.

The belt tightened infinitesimally as he finally sunk balls deep into her mouth. "*Fuck*," he ground out through clenched teeth. "You feel so good. Now concentrate. If you don't come before I do, you'll get another round with the ruler."

That snapped her out of the haze of sensation. Closing her eyes, she forced her hand to start moving, finally settling into a rhythm of her own. As Jonathan thrust in and out of her with increasing speed, she went faster as well, pressing down hard against the bundle of nerves, sending pleasure shooting through her body.

Fuck, he was so close. His movements became less measured, more erratic.

She began jerking her hand up and down, fast and hard enough to be painful. It was that sweet bite of pain that finally pushed her over the edge, mere seconds before Jonathan cried out, pushing all the way in as he came.

As pleasure rose inside of her, he yanked the belt tight enough to choke. Her whole body spasmed as her orgasm crested higher and higher, refusing to break.

Her eyes flew open as the pressure against her windpipe continued without reprieve. There was no fucking air. She was literally going to pass out.

And she'd never come this hard in her fucking life.

Just as the edges of her vision started to blur, the leather band disappeared from around her throat. Seconds later, Jonathn pulled free of her mouth. Only the hand still gripped tightly in her hair kept her from collapsing like a ragdoll on the floor.

"Eve." Her name fell from his lips like a prayer. Dropping to his knees, he gathered her into his arms, holding her tight against his chest. "My beautiful girl. You're fucking perfect."

CHAPTER 11

Jonathan

After their scene on the third floor, Eve fell deep into subspace. She remained conscious, but was in a dazed state, unable to move without his guidance, and though she occasionally spoke, it never made a whole lot of sense.

Rather than risk her taking a fall down the stairs, Jonathan scooped her into his arms, carrying her down to the master bedroom's en suite bathroom. He drew a bath in the enormous soaking tub, pouring some lavender oil into the steaming water. With any luck, the relaxing scent would help her come back to herself while the water soothed her body.

Climbing into the enormous soaking tub with her in his arms, he settled with his back against the sloped side, nestling her between his legs. He stayed with her there, one arm wrapped around her stomach, the other gently stroking her arm.

At least twenty minutes passed before one of her hands fanned out, curling gracefully through the water. "What happened?" she asked, still a little dazed, but finally sounding like herself again.

"You slipped into subspace," he explained, holding her closer against his chest.

"Subspace?" she repeated, muscles tensing. "What's that?"

He kept forgetting how much of a novice she was to a true BDSM lifestyle. That asshole Talley had no fucking clue what he was doing, and just used BDSM to justify abusing her. "Subspace happens sometimes when a ton of endorphins flood your system during a scene. It's almost like you go into a trance for a while." After a moment, he added, "I've been told it feels really good. I hope you enjoyed it."

The tension disappeared from her shoulders, and she relaxed back against him. "It felt like . . ." She trailed off as she searched for the right words. "Like I was floating. Like all the weight that's been pushing down on me as long as I can remember just lifted away. It was amazing."

His heart ached at her description—the weight pushing down on her. She deserved so much better than a life being crushed beneath unrelenting pressure.

Eve let out a huge yawn, slumping with exhaustion as soon as it finished.

"Come on, beautiful girl," he said, standing and helping her to her feet. "Let's get you to bed for a short nap. I have so many more plans for you this weekend, and I want you awake enough to enjoy them."

In response, she gave him a sleepy smile, looking him up and down as he helped her step out of the tub. "Ha, I win. I got to see you naked even though I didn't earn it."

Christ, she was adorable. Chuckling, Jonathan brushed a fingertip across the bruise already forming around her throat. "Trust me, you earned it."

An hour later, Jonathan sat in the old, gray armchair in the corner. He had his laptop balanced across his thighs and had made at least a cursory attempt at reviewing some paperwork Lainey emailed him that morning.

He couldn't concentrate worth a damn, though. Giving up altogether, he silently closed the screen, looking across the room at the woman sleeping in the center of the king-size bed. Her long hair fanned out around her, appearing black in the dim light—all except those vibrant red streaks. The ice pack he'd gotten to soothe the pain in her throat lay abandoned on the corner of the mattress.

This remarkable creature was his *girlfriend*. It still blew his mind. Even before he and the others founded Fairford Manor, he never dated —not exclusively anyway. He wasn't opposed to the idea, exactly. More like he'd just never found the time, his focus always zeroed in on something else.

First his education, where he'd done everything in his power to become valedictorian in high school, and then to graduate summa cum laude from college. He succeeded in both cases. Then came founding and running HSS Biotech, growing it from a tiny startup to a company that sold for just over a billion dollars seven years later.

And lastly, the Manor. His dream . . . the project of his heart. The impossible idea that came to him after a few too many tequila shots one night their senior year of college, which he'd somehow turned into a reality.

He'd built exactly the life he always wanted. But it wasn't until Eve called herself his girlfriend that he realized just how lonely it was, no matter how many people surrounded him every day, and most every night. For the first time, he thought maybe he wanted what the others had.

Leo and Sophie. Aiden and Olivia. Rafe and Nell. Mason and Addison. Zach and Remy.

And, of course, his parents. The single most perfect, loving couple he'd ever seen.

For the life of him, though, he couldn't figure out how any of them did it. How was he supposed to run the Manor, regularly take guests, solve everyone's problems for them, and still maintain a healthy relationship with this beautiful, fragile creature?

Standing, he tread softly across the floor, easing the door open and then back closed behind him. Eve didn't stir the entire time. Relieved, he hurried down the stairs and into the great room, settling onto the old, well-worn couch.

Jonathan got his phone out of his pocket, quickly pulling up his favorites list. His thumb hovered over Leo's name for several seconds, but ultimately, he hit *Dad* instead.

Orson Hale answered on the first ring. "Jonathan!" he said in greeting, his usually loud voice even higher in volume than normal. A lot of background noise filtered through the phone—loud voices and even louder music. "How are you?"

Instead of answering the question, he asked, "Where are you? It sounds loud as hell."

"Your mom and I are in San Diego for a Padres-Rockies game," he explained, sounding excited. "It's going to be hard rooting against the Rockies, but as the song says, root for the home team. We're hanging out at a bar near the ballpark until the gates open."

A smile found its way onto Jonathan's face. His parents had always loved baseball and had season tickets to both their favorite teams, since they spent so much time going between the two houses every summer. He had endless memories of attending games with them as a kid. "I don't want to be a bother—"

"No bother," Orson interrupted, his voice full of sincerity. "Let me just step outside for a minute." Muffled sounds came through the line as he made his way through what was clearly a crowded bar, lessening considerably when he finally made it outside. "There we go. That better?"

"Much. Thank you."

"Good, good." His dad chuckled. "I didn't mind all this craziness when I was younger, but I think I'm getting a little too old for this. But your mom insisted we come into town early."

Jonathan laughed, having no trouble picturing his mom dragging his dad to the car, her shoulder-length blond hair tucked up under a Padre's cap. The woman reveled in the pre-game energy of the bars near the ballpark.

"So what's up?" Orson asked.

"I'm hoping to get your advice on something."

"Is something wrong?" His voice had lost that jovial, laughing tone. "You don't sound too happy."

Jonathan thought about that for a second before he answered. "No, nothing's wrong. And I am happy. Maybe too happy? I don't know. It just feels like . . . like it can't possibly last. Does that make sense?"

His dad's chuckle came through the phone again. "Not even a little bit. You're going to have to give me some details here."

For a second, Jonathan considered saying never mind and ending the call. He was getting himself all worked up over nothing. All he had to do was enjoy the ride as he waited to see where this went.

Only problem with that was, sitting back and letting go of the controls came as naturally to Jonathan as breathing underwater.

"I've just started dating this woman," he forced himself to say. "And I'm really out of my depth here. I have no idea how to be in a relationship."

Orson didn't make a sound for so long, Jonathan would've thought the call dropped if he couldn't hear the bustle of the street. When at last he spoke, something like wonder filled his voice. "Are you telling me that you have a girlfriend?"

Jonathan rolled his eyes. "Yes, Dad, I have a girlfriend."

"Holy shit, did hell freeze over? Is the antichrist walking among us? Hold on." Scuffing sounds came through the line, soon joined by the bar music. "Lucy! *Lucy!* Come over here!"

"For God's sake, Dad," Jonathan grumbled, already regretting every choice in his life that brought him to this horrifying moment. One corner of his mouth moved up all on its own, despite his embarrassment.

Next thing Jonathan knew, his dad had put the phone on speaker, heightening the background noise. "What?" his mom asked, worry in her tone. "What's wrong?"

"Nothing's wrong," Orson assured her. "It's Jonathan on the phone. Tell her what you just told me."

"You've gotta be kidding me," Jonathan growled out, still fighting a smile.

"Oh, come on." His dad sounded like he was practically bouncing up and down with excitement. "Just tell her."

With another mighty roll of the eyes, he said, "Hi, Mom. Dad wants me to tell you that I have a girlfriend."

Lucy's shriek was so loud, he had to jerk the phone away from his ear. "I swear to God, if you two are playing a trick on me, I'll burn the pumpkin pie at every Thanksgiving until the day I die."

Jonathan laughed. He couldn't help it. "It's not a trick. I promise. Her name is Eve."

When his mother shrieked again, it didn't deafen him like last time, because he anticipated her reaction and pulled the phone away from his ear.

"Jesus, Mom, it's not that big a deal." Even as he said it, he knew it was bullshit.

"Jonathan Orson Hale, I gave up on you ever settling down long ago. At your own insistence, I might add. So do not try to tell me this is no big deal." A second later, she shouted, "My son has a girlfriend!" Drunken cheers answered this mortifying announcement, and he realized his mom had opened the bar door and yelled inside.

Thank fuck they were having this conversation on the phone. If he was there in San Diego with them, he might have dropped dead on the spot.

Orson's laugh had a nervous edge to it. "Why don't you head back inside and celebrate with everyone? We can call Jonathan in the morning to hear more about his new girl."

This idea clearly appealed to Lucy. "I'm happy for you, sweetheart!" she half-yelled into the phone. "Talk to you soon! Love you!" The bar music reappeared for a few seconds before thankfully fading away again.

"Sorry about that," his dad said, sounding equal parts amused and genuinely apologetic. "These twenty-two-year-olds from La Mesa have been buying her shots for the last hour."

Laughing again, Jonathan said, "Of course they have." His mother had the kind of magnetic personality that drew people to her. She was always making new friends in bars or on vacations.

"So you finally found a girl who could turn even your head." Orson whistled long and low. "She must be really special."

"She is." An understatement if ever there was one. "And I don't want to fuck this up. Since you and Mom are the best couple I know, I hoped you'd be able to give me some advice."

"My little boy all grown up and asking for dating advice," Orson said, sniffling dramatically. "I never thought this day would come."

Jonathan shook his head. "Dad, I'm thirty-eight," he said in the deadest, most unamused voice he could muster. "I've been all grown up for a very long time."

"Nope. You're not taking this moment away from me." More over-the-top sniffling came through the phone. "I've been patiently waiting for this moment since you hit puberty. Let me enjoy it."

"You're a pain in the ass."

"Thank you."

Jonathan chuckled. "Okay, you've had your moment. Get on with the advice giving."

"So bossy," Orson complained, though he sounded amused rather than upset. "I'm not one of your guests who you can order around, you know."

Snorting, Jonathan said, "Duly noted."

"All right, all right." He sounded more serious at last. "I'll stop torturing you. You came to the right place. I'm going to give you the best relationship advice you're ever going to get. Though it's maybe not as profound as you're hoping."

"Lay it on me."

"Communication and honesty."

Jonathan waited for him to say more, but the silence stretched on for several seconds. "That's it?"

"Son, if you have those two things down pat, the rest is easy." When he continued, he'd adopted a warning tone. "But you can't go partway on these. You have to be all in. I know that's never come easily to you."

Jonathan frowned at that. "I'm an excellent communicator." He'd run two successful businesses, for fuck's sake. How could he have accomplished that if he had poor communication skills?

"You're excellent at communicating exactly what you want other people to know." Orson said it kindly, but it was clear he wouldn't accept any arguments about this. "You need to learn how to communicate the rest of it—the parts you keep all to yourself."

It took three tries for Jonathan to swallow down the lump in his throat. "Got it."

"The honesty part is probably pretty self-explanatory," Orson said, and Jonathan was grateful for the subject change. "Without trust, love is impossible to sustain. Figure out some way to make sure you can completely trust each other. Knowing you can believe what your partner says no matter what makes all the difference in the world, believe me."

"What do you mean, figure out a way? Figure it out how?"

Orson clicked his tongue a few times—something he often did when thinking hard. "When we first got together, your mom and I had a word we'd say when one of us thought the other one was lying. It basically meant, this is really important, so tell me the truth no matter what. We both swore we'd never lie if the other person said that word, and neither of us ever did." He made a disappointed sound. "I can't remember what the word was. It's been over forty years since we've had to use it. Maybe she'll remember."

So there it was. The key to a forty-three-year marriage—communication and honesty.

It felt so simple. *Too* simple. Like those two things couldn't possibly solve every problem that came their way.

But it would sure be a great place to start.

"Thanks, Dad. I really appreciate it."

"My pleasure. Now I'd better get back in there before your mother starts dancing on the bar. Love you."

Jonathan smiled at the image of his sixty-eight-year-old mother dancing on a bar. It wasn't at all difficult to imagine. "Love you, too."

CHAPTER 12

Eve

Huddling deep within her orange Denver sweatshirt, Eve tucked her legs up under her on the oversize deck chair. It took a few tries to get everything situated just right, but she finally made the perfect blanket burrito around her legs, her exposed skin protected from the cool night air.

"No wonder you love it here so much," she said, leaning back against the plush cushion and closing her eyes. The chirps of crickets and other night insects mingled with the croaks of frogs. An owl call drifted in from somewhere out in the darkness—three short hoots followed by a longer one. Far off to their left, a second owl answered in the same pattern.

She was no stranger to the sounds of nature. Not in northern Vermont. But she could easily imagine how peaceful and beautiful a young Jonathan would've found this place when he spent most of his time in the chaotic bustle of southern California.

Jonathan stood on the edge of the large deck, leaning against the railing. For the first time since she'd met him, he had on a T-shirt instead of a button-down and tie. His dark gray sweats were doing wonderful things for his ass, especially with him bent over like that.

Keep it in your pants, Eve, she scolded, not wanting to ruin this beautiful moment.

"My dad and I used to sit out here after everyone else went to bed," he said, his voice taking on that misty, faraway quality again. "Just the two of us. We've both always been night owls. I'm sure everyone knew we were out here, but it always felt like our secret. Like our own special club or something." His sigh held so many emotions, from gratitude to longing to regret. "We haven't done anything like that for years."

Eve was glad he faced away from her and couldn't see her brush tears from her eyes. She remembered nights like that with her dad when she was growing up. Unlike Jonathan, she never had to wait for the rest of the family to go to bed. It had been just the two of them as long as she could remember.

Staying up way too late, raiding the pantry and the freezer at two AM, talking about anything and everything. She couldn't even remember what they'd talked about anymore—most of it was nonsense anyway.

But she'd never forget how those nights made her feel.

Like she mattered. Like she wasn't and never would be alone.

In those moments, she knew, without a doubt, that she was the most important person in his world. Just as he was the most important person in hers.

Sixteen years had gone by since she lost him. In all that time, the depth of her longing for one more night with him hadn't diminished one bit.

"Are you still close to your dad?" she asked, hoping despite a slight spark of envy that he'd answer yes. She wouldn't wish her situation on anyone, least of all a person who she'd come to care for deeply.

"Very close," he said, and her heart filled with happiness for him. "I'm about to turn forty, and he's still the person I go to for advice when I need it most." He chuckled, looking over his shoulder at her. "I hope that doesn't make me sound pathetic."

It took her a few seconds to answer. She had to swallow three times to make the lump in her throat disappear. "I think it makes you sound lucky."

One side of his mouth lifted into a small smile just before he turned back toward the darkness. "Will you tell me about your dad?" he asked, tone gentle. He kept his back to her, as if he knew she wouldn't want him to see her tears. She appreciated his kindness more than she knew how to express.

"He was funny. That's what I remember most about being with him —how much we both laughed." She closed her eyes for a moment, picturing his laughing face. "He was the kind of person who could diffuse even the tensest, shittiest situation. Someone could be ready to fight him one minute, and then cracking up the next." That literally happened once, when he had to fire one of his employees. The two still sent each other Christmas cards for years afterward. "It made him an amazing boss. The crew adored him."

"I'm sorry you didn't have him in your life longer," Jonathan said, so softly that she barely heard him over the noise of the forest. "He sounds like an incredible man. No wonder you're so amazing." At this, he finally turned back around, his eyes boring into hers. It wasn't lust she saw there now, though the heat in his eyes still seemed to scorch her.

Eve had known for a while that she wanted him, and for almost as long that she respected him as a person. But as this magical day progressed, she found her feelings changing. Deepening into something she didn't have a name for yet.

"Jonathan, I—"

The loud buzz of his cell phone interrupted her. "Shit, I'm sorry," he said, fishing it out of his pocket. When he saw the screen, he gave her an apologetic look. "It's my sister Maisie. She usually texts, and only ever calls if it's really important. Do you mind if I—"

"Answer it," she said without hesitation. "I don't mind." She had no doubt that if she had a family to call her, he'd be just as understanding.

With a grateful smile, he turned back around, leaning against the railing before bringing the phone up to his ear. "Hey, Maise. What's up?"

Settling back in the chair, Eve looked out into the trees, happy for a chance to think before they continued their conversation. So much had happened in the last thirty hours or so, and she hadn't yet had a chance to wrap her head around all of it.

Jonathan straightened so abruptly, she yelped in surprise. "*What?*"

Bewilderment saturated his voice. In that single word, he sounded utterly lost.

Eve fought her way out of the tangled blanket, launching herself from the chair and across the porch. "What is it? What's wrong?"

Not even seeming to hear her, Jonathan held the phone against his ear in a death grip. "I—I don't . . ." He didn't sound a thing like himself, the words hollow, his usual confidence and strength nowhere to be found.

The phone fell from his hand, clattering against the ground. "Jonathan, what—shit!" His legs gave out, and she caught him as best she could, getting his arm wrapped around her shoulders. "Come on," she said, half-dragging him toward the chair she'd abandoned as best she could. "That's it."

It took some major finagling, especially given how much taller and heavier he was than her. She was out of breath by the time she helped him through a semi-controlled collapse into the chair. Squatting down between his legs, she grabbed his hands, trying to get him to look at her. His skin was cold as ice. "Jonathan? What's happening? What can I do?"

His unfocused eyes stared in the vague direction of her face, but he didn't seem to see her at all.

Not sure what else to do, she ran back across the porch, snatching his phone up off the floor. Thank God the call hadn't ended; she could hear the person on the other end screaming Jonathan's name. "Hello? What's going on? I think Jonathan's in shock or something."

"Oh, thank fuck," the woman said, literally crying with relief. "I thought he was alone. Can you help him? Who is this?"

"Eve." Realizing that probably meant nothing to Jonathan's sister, she added, "His girlfriend."

Maisie was silent for a few seconds. "Girlfriend," she repeated, genuine wonder in her voice. "He's never had a girlfriend before."

"Not important right now," Eve said, trying to get the woman back on track. "What's going on? What do I need to do?"

The sound of crying came through the phone again. "I'm his sister, Maisie," she said, struggling to get the words out through her tears.

"Our dad—he's—he—" She dissolved into a fit of sobs, unable to say anything more.

Eve's whole body went numb. *No. Please God, don't do this to him.*

"This is Maisie's husband, Sean," a new voice said. Though grief filled each word, he at least wasn't crying. "I'm so sorry we have to meet this way." He sighed. "Jonathan and Maisie's dad had a heart attack an hour ago. Their mom gave him CPR while she waited for the paramedics to get here, but there was nothing any of them could do. He passed on before they arrived."

CHAPTER 13
Jonathan

The next thirty-six hours passed by in a dense fog. Bits and pieces stuck out in Jonathan's mind, more like snapshots than actual memories. Eve holding his phone up to his face to unlock it. Eve behind the wheel of Maisie's Jeep. Eve holding his hand on the jet.

Eve.

Everything came down to Eve.

When he woke up late Sunday morning in his childhood bedroom, long since repurposed into a guest room, he had only the vaguest notion of how he got there. Someone—presumably Eve—had stripped him down to his boxer briefs. The suit he wore most of Friday hung in the open closet to his right, and his sweatpants and T-shirt were neatly folded on the chair in the corner.

Sitting up, he noticed a large glass of water, two granola bars, and a bottle of ibuprofen on the nightstand. Next to them sat a single sheet of lined paper. The left edge still held jagged remnants from being ripped out of a spiral notebook.

Jonathan,

First, let me tell you how deeply sorry I am for what's happened. If you need me for literally anything, I'm right downstairs. Just call or text.

I haven't been able to get you to eat or drink much since Friday night. If you can, try to drink this whole glass, and eat whatever you're able. I got you some Advil too, because I'm sure you're really dehydrated, and that always gives me a massive headache.

If you're feeling up for it, come downstairs. I'll make you some real food while you spend some time with your family. But if not, everyone understands. I promise. Take all the time you need.

Love,

Eve

He blinked at the note a few times, trying to piece together what had happened since he got the phone call.

That phone call.

Giving up the time as lost for good, he opened the pill bottle, popping two into his mouth. As instructed, he downed the entire glass of water. The granola bars still untouched, he forced himself to stand and start dressing with slow, almost mechanical movements.

He managed to get the suit and shoes on, but his fingers fumbled with the tie both times he tried. His movements felt slow and clumsy, almost like his brain and body weren't quite in sync. With a sigh, he draped the striped, blue silk back over a hanger, returning it to the closet.

Closing his eyes, he stood in the center of the room and just breathed. He could do this. He could fucking do it. His family needed him, and he'd let them down for long enough already. Time to step up and do what needed to be done.

How could he do that when he'd gone completely numb?

"Goddamnit, Jonathan," he said through clenched teeth. "Get your shit together."

With one more deep breath that did absolutely nothing, he opened his eyes and stepped out into the hall.

Somber voices drifted up the staircase from below, too low to make out any words. His body froze, muscles and joints all locking into place. Panic filled his mind, his chest—a physical, pulsating thing inside of him. More than anything, he desperately wished to flee back into his room and lock the door behind him.

"Goddamnit, Jonathan," he said again, breathing through it, pushing the feelings down, down, down, until they became small enough to ignore. Straightening his shoulders, he walked down the stairs.

As soon as he entered the living room, Maisie launched herself off the couch, slamming into his chest with enough force to knock the breath from his lungs. She didn't say a word. Simply wrapped her arms around him and cried into his already crumpled white shirt.

His mind went completely blank for several seconds. By the time he realized he should hug her back, he knew far too much time had already passed. Everyone else in the room watched—his other sister Alice, his brothers-in-law, his mom, and even his three nephews.

All eyes on him, waiting for him to comfort his baby sister. To say something. Literally anything.

His gaze slid over to Eve, who sat in one of the chairs by the fireplace with Maisie's five-month-old daughter on her lap. She wasn't judging him. Wasn't looking to him, expecting him to provide all the answers.

She worried about him and wanted to help. Nothing more.

Having Eve on his side gave him the strength he needed to wrap his arms around Maisie's shoulders, holding her close. "It's going to be okay," he said softly. "We'll figure out how to get through this. Together."

If only he could believe it himself.

"Jonathan, can you help me please?" His mother stood at the entryway to the kitchen in a simple black dress with powder blue flowers around the hem.

He missed her usual colorful, flamboyant style, and found himself hoping it wasn't gone for good. "Sure." Putting his coffee mug on the counter, he kissed Eve on the temple. "I'll be back."

Lucy led him through the house and upstairs, moving straight into the master bedroom. "Eve is lovely," she said, voice soft and subdued, as she headed for the walk-in closet. "She's so sweet, especially with the kids. Maisie and Alice love her already."

His two younger sisters had already told him as much, cornering him when he went to the bathroom earlier. "Thank you," he said—the same response he'd given the other two. He knew it was deeply inadequate, but it felt so surreal. So entirely wrong for Eve to meet his family this way. To hear how wonderful she was when a cloud of grief hung over them all, low and thick and suffocating.

How could he possibly find the words and the strength to express how much Eve meant to him when his heart was breaking?

Lucy looked up at him for several seconds, a searching look in her eyes. He stared back impassively, not sure what else to do.

Sighing, she stepped into the closet and turned on the light. "I need to take Orson's suit to the funeral home this afternoon. You know more about suits than the rest of us combined, so I thought you should probably choose."

Jonathan froze on the threshold of the closet, staring at the row of suits behind his mother. She couldn't be serious. No way could she really be asking him to choose the suit his dad would be buried in.

No, no, no, no, no.

She began examining the suits one at a time, sliding each one down the rack when she finished with it. "I talked to the girls last night, and we all think you should give the eulogy," she went on, completely oblivious to what was going on behind her.

Panic exploded through him again, making his chest so tight and painful that he couldn't breathe.

"The Episcopal funeral service usually doesn't have one, but Uncle Warren is Catholic, and he got really upset when I told him. He's already furious we're doing it at our church instead of his." She rolled her eyes. "So I talked to the priest, and she said it was okay. You're the best public speaker by far, and you're the only one who will really do it justice."

What the fuck what the fuck what the fuck...

Those words spiraled through his mind again and again, pushing out his ability to think.

"Jonathan."

He jerked back as if he'd been slapped. His mom had half-shouted his name, and he got the impression this wasn't the first time she said it. Blinking several times until his vision came back into proper focus, he drew in a shaky breath. "I'm sorry." He wasn't sure what else to say.

Lucy placed a soft hand on his shoulder. "Sweetheart, you have nothing to be sorry for. This isn't easy for any of us."

And yet, he was the only one completely losing his shit. How could he not? Why was everyone else so much calmer about this?

"I talked to him that afternoon, only hours before . . ." Jonathan pushed out a jagged sigh. He couldn't bring himself to finish the sentence. "I don't understand what happened. He was perfectly fine. He's always been perfectly fine."

Orson Hale had one of those magical immune systems where he hardly ever got sick, even so much as a cold. He played squash twice a week and had been obsessed with his Peloton bike ever since the shutdown in 2020. Nothing about this made any fucking sense.

Tears glistened in his mom's eyes, making him feel like a complete asshole. Dealing with his bullshit was the last thing she needed right now.

"I'm sorry," he said again, inching around her in the packed closet and moving toward the row of suits. "Let me take a look at these." He reached for the first one, ready to do this for her no matter how much it tore him up inside, but her hand on his arm stopped him.

"Sweetheart. Look at me."

Swallowing down the lump once again threatening to choke him, he turned.

"Sometimes these things just don't make sense. You hear about vegans who run marathons getting cancer in their forties. Then there are people like your great-grandfather, who smoked two packs a day and basically stayed drunk for the last forty years of his life, and he died peacefully in his bed at ninety-three. There's only so much we can control."

"But I'm not ready for this," Jonathan admitted, finally making himself say the words out loud. For the first time, hot tears splashed against his cheeks. "I'm not remotely fucking ready."

Lucy's face crumpled for only a moment or two, but she wiped the new tears away, standing tall and strong before him. "I'm not either," she whispered. "But we have to figure out how to get ready pretty damn quick, sweetheart, because God didn't give us a choice on this one."

This time, his body knew what to do all on its own. He wrapped his arms around his mother, holding her close as they both gave in to their tears.

Jonathan still had no idea how to handle any of it by the time people began arriving at the church four days later. But with Eve's help, he at least figured out how to pretend enough to get through it.

"No one expects you to act like everything's okay," she told him earlier that morning, as he donned one of the suits Zach overnighted from Vermont. "So you need to stop trying, or you're going to completely break."

"Don't they, though?" Jonathan said, flipping up the collar of his stiff, white shirt, looping a somber grey tie behind his neck. "I'm supposed to give the eulogy. The fucking *eulogy*. If I screw this up, they'll never forgive me."

When his hands couldn't muster the fine motor skills to knot his tie for the fifth day in a row, she stepped in and did it for him. "I gave the eulogy at my dad's funeral, too," she said, voice haunted by the long-ago memory. "It was the hardest thing I've ever done."

"How did you get through it?" Desperation clung to the question—

a plea to save him from what he was sure would end up being the biggest failure of his life.

She thought about it as she finished adjusting his tie and popped his collar down into place. When at last she answered, she sounded almost wistful. "I realized I wasn't giving the eulogy for other people. I was giving it for me."

Frowning, Jonathan admitted, "I don't understand."

"It didn't need to be this perfect, beautiful speech. I wasn't being graded, and I wasn't some politician trying to win people over to my side. Everyone was already on my side." Reaching up, she straightened his hair, putting it back to the way he liked it. He really needed to stop running his hands through it so often. "Once I realized that, I knew all I needed to do was say what would be helpful to me."

"But how am I supposed to know what that is?" he asked, fucking up his hair before he realized what he was doing.

Her sad little smile as she fixed his hair again soothed the pain in his chest the tiniest bit. "It might be something different for you. But for me, it helped to talk about all the best times I ever had with my dad. Forcing myself to say it out loud helped me remember how lucky I was to have him in the first place." She shrugged, an almost apologetic look in her dark eyes. "And I guess it kind of tricked my brain into forgetting what a fucking wreck I was. Long enough to get through the funeral anyway."

Now here he was, shaking hands and hugging people as they filed solemnly into the church, saying, "Thank you," over and over again as they offered their condolences. And in the back of his mind, he ran through the best memories he had of his father, like his own personal home video montage.

When a large group of people from the Manor appeared at the open double doors, he almost lost his resolve. If Eve hadn't put her hand in his at that moment, drawing him out of his racing thoughts, he may well have broken down. Instead, he steeled his nerves and approached his closest friends in the world.

"What are you doing here?" he asked, hearing how utterly grateful and bewildered he sounded. He held his hand out to Leo, his oldest friend, who hauled him into a hug instead.

"What kind of question is that," Leo said in his ear, letting Jonathan lean on him until he got himself under enough control to pull away. "We all wanted to be here for you."

"But the Manor—"

"Will survive if we close it down for a couple days and reschedule a few people," Rafe interrupted in his deep, gruff voice.

Camden hurried to add, "All the guests understood." For once, his fuckboy grin was nowhere to be found.

Blinking back tears, Jonathan hugged Aiden next, and then Olivia. "You're supposed to be in Bali." The two still hadn't taken a proper vacation since they got married over a year ago. "I can't believe you left your honeymoon for this."

"You're a hell of a lot more important to us than a fucking trip," Aiden said, the threat of tears already heavy in his voice.

"And you know how much we all loved your dad," Mason said, the usual icy intensity of his deep blue eyes replaced by a compassion rarely seen in the man. For only the second time in over twenty-five years of friendship, Mason hugged him. "We're all here for you, literally anything you need. That's a promise."

Jonathan had to wipe away tears as Mason pulled away, and Zach handed him a handkerchief before he could retrieve one from his own pocket. A bright orange poppy had been embroidered into one corner, a lavender and white columbine into the corner opposite. The state flowers of California and Colorado, he realized with a start.

When he tried to hand the handkerchief back after dabbing at his eyes, Zach waved him away. "Keep it. I made it for you."

At Jonathan's surprised look, Remy pulled another handkerchief from his pocket, holding it out so he could see the red and orange hibiscus flowers artfully arranged around one corner. "He got bored with calligraphy and took up embroidery last winter. Our house looks like an old lady lives there."

Before he knew it was coming, Jonathan huffed out a short laugh. His eyes widened at the sound. How was laughter even possible on a day like today?

Zach hurried forward and flung his arms around Jonathan, not giving him the chance to fall too deeply down that rabbit hole. "I'm so, so sorry," Zach said as Jonathan hugged the man's slender shoulders. "You need anything at all, you call me first, okay? You had my back when I needed it most, and now I have yours, no matter what."

For the life of him, he couldn't figure out why it astounded him that they'd all come. He turned that over in his mind as he accepted hugs and condolences from Remy, Sophie, Rafe, Nell, Addison, and Camden in turn.

The group shuffled off to find seats, Camden stopping to whisper something in Eve's ear on his way by. Eve moved up beside him after they were gone, slipping her hand into his.

"What did he say to you?" Jonathan asked.

She gave his hand a little squeeze. "He said, 'Jonathan is like my brother. Thank you for being with him through all this.'"

Tears welled in Jonathan's eyes yet again, and he blinked them away.

"Remember, you're not alone," she said softly, leaning her head against his shoulder. "Not like I was. We're all here for you, no matter what."

Knowing all the people he cared about most in this world were right here in this church carried him through the rest of the arrivals.

When it came time for everyone to take their seats, Eve tried to sit with the Manor group near the back of the church. "I think it would be more appropriate," she whispered as she attempted to pull away.

He didn't let go of her hand. "Please sit with me," he said, letting his fear show on his face for only a moment. "I don't think I can do this alone."

Her eyes melted, and she nodded without hesitation. They took their seats in the front row, between his mom and Alice. Neither of the women looked surprised to see Eve at his side.

Most of the funeral passed in a blur, the priest reading several bible verses that he only half paid attention to. Despite being raised by moderately religious parents, Jonathan was agnostic at best—not against the idea of a God per se, just not convinced either. His mother had been the one who wanted a proper religious funeral, in the Episcopal church his parents attended since moving to this corner of California in their early twenties.

When at last the priest announced it was time for Jonathan to give his eulogy, his legs felt almost too weak to stand.

"It's okay," Eve whispered as he wiped his suddenly clammy hands on his slacks. "Remember, everyone's already on your side."

Bolstered by her words, he managed to rise to his feet and button his jacket. Holding his spine straight and his head high, he walked up to the lectern. He could do this. Not for all the people out there, but for himself.

He needed to say goodbye.

"Thank you everyone for being here to support our family today." He cleared his throat, wishing he had a glass of water. "My father was . . . he was . . ." He swallowed, trying to force the lump in his throat down again, but this time it wouldn't go away. Christ, he was going to start crying up here and completely fail this whole fucking thing, disappointing everyone.

But when he looked out at the gathered crowd, he didn't see a single angry or disappointed face. Alice leaned against Dillon, her husband, watching Jonathan with the same stoic expression she'd worn since he arrived in California. For as long as he could remember, she didn't like to show too much negative emotion when other people could see. Even so, she clutched a tissue in one hand.

Maisie, who had been crying for the last half hour, continued to wipe at her nose and eyes with the endless stream of tissues Sean provided for her. She watched him with shining eyes, grief and hope making up equal parts of her expression.

Then there was Eve. Her beautiful eyes held nothing but support and her unwavering belief that he could do this.

It was his mom's expression that affected him most of all, though. She, too, had been crying for most of the service. But now she looked at him with so much pride that it strengthened his weakened body, resolved his mind.

Pulling the embroidered handkerchief from his pocket, he pressed it against his eyes one at a time, gathering his tears. And then he started to speak.

"My father was the funniest, most laid-back man I've ever known. I have no idea how I happened, because I'm pretty sure I came out of

Mom's uterus wearing a suit." A chuckle rolled through the pews, and his mother smiled for a moment. "But that never bothered Dad. He didn't tell me to relax, or act more like he did at my age, or that I'd give myself an ulcer before I turned twenty-five." He paused, then admitted, "Okay, maybe he said the ulcer part." More laughter.

"But my point is, he never tried to change me. *Never.* Even when I made some rather unorthodox choices these last ten years, he always embraced exactly who I am. Do you have any idea how lucky that makes me?" He looked over at his sisters, meeting each of their gazes in turn. "How lucky it makes all three of us?

"No matter what we did, we always had someone to go to for support and advice. Someone who wouldn't judge us or condemn us or tell us we were out of our minds. If one of us told him we wanted to reach for the stars, he asked how he could help build the spaceship every single time."

Alice's stony exterior finally cracked, and she buried her face against Dillon's shoulder, whole body shaking with her tears.

"Losing my dad has left a hole in me I can't even begin to fill. Perhaps if we'd known it was coming—if we had time to . . . to say good-bye." He wiped fresh tears from his eyes as he fought to regain his voice. "But I keep reminding myself that I had over thirty-eight years for this man to teach me. For him to love me and show me how to love others. For him to make me laugh when I got too serious. Not everyone gets that."

He looked at Eve, who lost her dad at such a young age. Then at Aiden and Rafe, whose parents wanted nothing to do with them anymore. At Olivia, who ran away from her abusive home at eighteen and never looked back. He didn't know much about Addison's story yet, but he knew enough to know her childhood hadn't been a bed of roses either, though she'd recently connected with her biological dad for the first time.

"My dad was the most wonderful man I've ever known, and I'll miss him every single day for the rest of my life. But I'm also going to use everything he taught me to make that life the best one I possibly can." He met Maisie's eyes again, and then Alice's. "I know, beyond a shadow of a doubt, Dad would want that for us. He'd want to know that he left behind a legacy of joy. Of acceptance and peace and love. We can give him that."

He looked out over the whole congregation. "We all can. When you leave this place today, try to remember something Orson Hale taught you. Remember a time he cheered you up with a ridiculous story when you were having a bad day. Or remember a time he showed up for you, even if maybe no one else did. And try to put that kind of energy out into the world. It'll be a better place because of it."

CHAPTER 14

Eve

Sitting alone at a table near the back of the event hall, Eve did her best to be invisible. Not that she disliked any of the people here at the luncheon. Jonathan's family had welcomed her as one of their own without question, especially his mom and sisters. And, of course, she already knew the people who had arrived from the Manor, to varying degrees.

No, she hid in the corner because the more she heard about Orson Hale, the more he reminded her of her own dad. After so many years, she thought she'd completely worked through her grief. But hearing story after story that could just as easily have been told at her dad's funeral made it abundantly clear she was wrong.

She'd go back out there in a few minutes, after a short break.

For at least the tenth time since that morning, she went over Jonathan's eulogy in her mind. She didn't think she'd ever heard anything more beautiful in her life.

Eve had no choice but to admit it, to herself at least. She fell just a little bit in love with him while he stood behind that podium, revealing his fractured heart to the other hurting people around him.

A tall man, broad shouldered man who appeared to be in his sixties or early seventies walked up to her table. He dropped into the chair next to her without waiting for an invitation. "I hear you're dating my nephew," he said, not bothering to introduce himself first.

Oh, for fuck's sake. She only wanted a few minutes to herself. Was that too much to ask?

Summoning up the dregs of her dwindling energy supplies, she held out her hand. "I'm Eve. You must be Orson's brother." The man bore a remarkable resemblance to the pictures of Jonathan's father she'd seen the last few days. He'd also been one of the pallbearers, standing just behind Jonathan.

"Warren Hale." He shook her hand only once before letting go.

She remembered Alice making some offhand comment about her Uncle Warren—how he threw a hissy fit about where the funeral would be held. Fuck, she wished Jonathan or one of his sisters was here to carry on the bulk of the conversation. It had been stupid to try to slip off on her own. "I'm so sorry for your loss," she said awkwardly, "From everything I've heard, it sounds like Orson was an incredible man."

Warren tilted his head slightly to one side. "You didn't know him?"

Something in the man's tone set off a warning in her head, though she wasn't sure why. She decided to remain as polite as possible and hope it was her imagination. "I unfortunately didn't get the chance to meet him. I really wish I had."

"How long have you and Jonathan been dating?"

Oh yeah, it definitely wasn't her imagination. She had no doubt that he'd react poorly to the true answer to that question. "Not long," she said noncommittally.

"And yet you sat in the first pew with Jonathan and the girls," he said, tone making it abundantly clear what he thought about that. His eyes narrowed almost imperceptibly as the silence stretched out.

"Jonathan wanted me there," she said at last, not liking the direction of this conversation at all. The hairs on the back of her neck stood on end. "I want to support him, and all of you, any way I can. Now if you'll excuse me, I need to get back to Jonathan. It was nice meeting you."

She scurried away faster than was strictly polite, but she didn't care about that anymore. The way he looked at her made her instincts kick into high gear. If she had to walk past him alone in a parking lot, she'd put her keys between her fingers in case she had to go all Wolverine on his ass.

Eve nearly made it back to the table where Jonathan sat with various members of his family when Warren caught up. "Those are interesting bruises around your neck," Warren said just a tad too loud, eyeing the band left by Jonathan's belt with raised brows. "I wonder how you got those."

The jerk clearly had no intention of letting it drop. He'd cause a scene whether she participated willingly or not. Cheeks heating with a betraying blush, she turned to face the older man. "That's none of your business."

"But it is yours, right?" At her confused look, he said, "Your business, I mean. I assume you work at that hotel of his. I must say, bringing a prostitute to his own father's funeral is a bit too far, even for him."

Eve's mouth fell open, her mind going completely blank. How in the fuck was she supposed to respond to that?

Before she could figure it out, Lucy Hale stood at her side. The woman leveled her brother-in-law with a death glare that would've sent her running. "Shut your damn mouth, Warren. One more remark out of you and I'm going to ask you to leave."

Jonathan moved up to Eve's other side, putting a protective hand on her shoulder. "What's going on?"

"Eve was just telling me about her work at that little hotel of yours," Warren said, a cruel glint to his eyes.

Frowning, Jonathan looked down at Eve and his mother, then back up at his uncle. "Eve has been working in construction her whole life. She's absolutely brilliant. The whole project would be a mess without her."

It was Warren's turn to frown. He opened his mouth, closed it again, and then began fidgeting with the buttons on his suit jacket.

"Jonathan's *little hotel* is doing so well, they've had to expand," Lucy said, looping her arm through Eve's. "As I understand it, this lovely young lady here is one of the two people leading the whole team. We've all been enjoying learning more about her accomplishments."

Warren continued to look uncomfortable for a few more seconds, but he rallied quickly enough, that cold, hateful glint back in his eyes.

"Oh, get your nose out of the air, Lucy. Your boy runs a sex hotel, for heaven's sake. And I'm sure you've noticed the bruises all over the girl. Did you raise your son to hit women, or was that Orson's doing?"

By the time he finished speaking, the entire room had gone silent. As if this needed to be any more mortifying.

"Fuck off, Warren," Jonathan said, the hand on her shoulder shaking with rage. "As usual, you have no idea what you're talking about."

Warren gave Lucy another superior look. "It was definitely you who taught him not to respect his elders."

She glared back at her brother-in-law. "No, it was me who taught him he only has to show respect when it's been earned."

A few people Eve didn't recognize walked cautiously up to the group. One middle-aged brunette woman had her hands out in front of her, like she was approaching a stray dog and didn't want to startle it into biting her. "Why don't we all calm down," she said in the most kindergarten teacher voice Eve had ever heard. "Dad, let's go for a walk."

Warren glowered at the woman who was apparently his daughter. "You're telling *me* to leave?"

"You're out of line, Uncle Warren," Alice said, moving up to stand at Jonathan's other side.

"I just had to listen to a goddamn pimp give the eulogy at my brother's funeral, and you're telling me *I'm* out of line?" He barked out a callous laugh, then looked Jonathan right in the eyes. "Orson was ashamed of you. He would've wanted me to give the eulogy."

"That's a lie," Lucy said, hands fisted at her sides, every muscle in her body rigid. "Orson was so proud of all three of our children, as am I. They're all happy and being true to who they really are. What decent parent would want more than that for their kids?"

Scoffing, Warren shoved a finger toward the center of Jonathan's chest. "Proud? After all the shit this one put him through, it's no wonder he had a heart attack."

Without any warning at all, Jonathan drew his hand back and punched his uncle in the face. For the space of a heartbeat, everything went completely silent and still, as if a spell fell over the room.

A second later, it all devolved into chaos.

"Jonathan!" Eve yelled, and she wasn't the only one. She and Alice both tried to grab onto him as he advanced on Warren, but he pulled out of their grasps as easily as if their hands were made of smoke.

"You son of a bitch!" Warren roared, holding a hand over his nose, blood slipping through his fingers. "Get this maniac away from me. You all saw him attack me. Call the police."

"Jonathan, stop!" Maisie ran up, holding her daughter on her hip. "Who cares what that asshole thinks?"

Ignoring all of them, Jonathan grabbed a fistful of his uncle's shirt, hauling him up from where he'd toppled to the ground. But before he could get another punch in, Leo and Aiden leapt into the fray, grabbing his arms and pulling him back. "Come on, man," Leo said, struggling to keep his grip as Jonathan fought to get away. "It's not worth it. You know it's not."

For a moment, it looked as if Jonathan would break away from them. But then Rafe and Camden arrived. The two men looked as though they could bench press Jonathan if they wanted and had no trouble hauling him away from his uncle and outside.

Eve ran after them, the rest of the Fairford Manor crew right on her heels.

As soon as they pushed through the doors and out into the sunlight, Jonathan wrenched away from the other two men. This time, they let him go, and he stalked off several steps, letting out something halfway between a scream and a growl.

"Jesus, Jonathan," Leo said as he hurried through the doors. "I know the guy's an asshole, but come on. It's your dad's funeral. Get it together."

"Did you hear what he said?" Jonathan demanded, keeping his back to them.

Sighing, Leo said, "Yeah, he called you a pimp and said a bunch of stupid shit about Eve. He's not the first to say ignorant shit like that, and I'm sure he won't be the last. The moron has no idea what he's talking about."

Eve held her breath. That wasn't what set him off. Not even close.

"No," Jonathan forced out between clenched teeth. "He said I killed my dad. He said it's my fault he had a heart attack."

Everyone except Eve tensed, all at once.

She stepped forward slowly, wanting to give him plenty of time to ask her to stop. When he didn't say anything or move away, she placed a tentative hand on his shoulder.

Jonathan shoved the hand away. "Don't touch me right now." So much anguish filled those words. "*Please.* I'm too angry. I don't want to hurt you."

"Okay," she said softly, resisting the urge to fiddle with her ring. "But I'm here, and I'm not going anywhere. I'm not afraid you'll hurt me."

"I already hurt you." He gasped out a strangled half-sob. "My whole fucking family thinks I hurt you."

"And that," Aiden said in a kind, level voice, "is none of their goddamn business." He moved up beside her, but ventured no closer, careful to give Jonathan his space. "Our subs have the power to stop us with a single word. Just because some prejudiced Neanderthal doesn't get it doesn't make it untrue."

Mason took position at Eve's other side, looming almost a foot taller than her. "There are seven Doms and six subs out here right now. And I guarantee you every single one of us has more kindness and respect in our pinky finger than your uncle has in his whole body."

"Don't let him make you ashamed of who you are," Eve said, almost pleading. "There's something my dad used to say all the time. You should never take criticism from someone you wouldn't go to for advice." She thought of how deeply she'd failed at that since her father died, resolving to do better from now on.

"I wouldn't even ask that guy for a restaurant recommendation," Zach said. "I sure as fuck wouldn't let him tell me how to live my life."

Just then, the doors opened behind them, and she turned in time to see his mom and sisters come outside. Maisie must have handed her daughter off to Sean. "Uncle Warren's gone," Maisie said, taking in the strained gathering with worried eyes. "When he realized no one was on his side, he stopped all his bullshit about calling the police and slunk out the back door."

"I'm so sorry, sweetheart," Lucy added. "You shouldn't have had to go through that. Especially not today of all days."

None of the tension eased out of Jonathan's body, but he did finally manage to turn. "Thank you. All of you. You're the people I care most about in the world. I appreciate you having my back."

It took Eve a moment to realize he included her in that group. *The people I care most about in the world.*

She fell a little bit deeper.

"Now if you'll excuse me," he continued, sounding almost robotic now. "I think I'll take a walk before I come back inside. Not giving anyone a chance to respond, he turned and strode away, shoulders stiff and tense, his hands shoved in his pockets.

Eve's chest ached as she watched him go. She longed for something she could do to ease his pain—to take away this current desire to be on his own. If it was in her power, she'd do anything to make that happen.

Resolve flowed through her as she followed the others back inside. This wasn't a time for impotent hopes and worries. Not when Jonathan so clearly required her help.

What she needed was a plan.

CHAPTER 15

Jonathan

W hat a fucking mess. The rest of the memorial luncheon passed in awkward near-silence, people staring at him and Eve whenever they thought he wasn't looking. In the end, everyone gave up and went home early. Even his mom and sisters.

What was supposed to be a celebration of his father's life turned into a giant clusterfuck.

Eve held his hand as he drove back to Del Mar, her thumb moving back and forth across his skin in a constant, calming rhythm.

"I want to help you," she said, breaking the silence after more than fifteen minutes.

"You are helping me." She hadn't left his side once since he returned to the event hall. He couldn't think of anything more helpful than that.

Looking over at him from the passenger seat, she studied his face for several seconds. "Not nearly enough," she said, shaking her head. "You need to let off some steam before you explode."

Jonathan's heart skipped a beat. "What do you mean by that?"

She placed her free hand on his arm, wrapping her warm fingers around his bicep. "You know exactly what I mean by that."

A ragged breath forced its way out of him. He wanted what she was offering. He wanted it so fucking badly. "I don't think it's a good idea." It almost killed him to say it.

"I trust you."

"You shouldn't."

"Yes, I should." There wasn't a trace of doubt in her voice. "I can give you what you need. Use me to make yourself feel better."

He pushed out a harsh sigh. "Eve, you can't handle that yet."

"Yes, I can," she insisted. "Let me show you."

He hesitated for a little longer, two sides of him at war. It felt like those cartoons where a little angel appeared on one shoulder, while a devil whispered sweet temptations from the other.

The devil won.

Jerking the steering wheel, he swerved across two lanes of the I-5, cutting across the median between the highway and the exit ramp.

"Fuck!" Eve shouted, grabbing the oh-shit handle and holding on for dear life. "What the hell are you—*oh*." She'd seen the look in his eyes.

She didn't say another word as he maneuvered the car onto CA-56, driving faster than entirely advisable. Nine minutes later, as he left highways behind, she sat perfectly straight in her seat, gaze moving from side to side, on the lookout for their mystery destination.

When he pulled through the front gates of the sprawling, Mediterranean-style hotel a few minutes later, her hand jerked in his. Her eyes went wide as she took in the pink stucco walls, red tiled roofs, and high archways.

Jonathan pulled up to the valet stand, handing the car key and a fifty-dollar bill to the young man who rushed out to greet him. "Hold the car here until I come back," he instructed. "I shouldn't be more than ten minutes."

As soon as the kid noticed the fifty in his hand, he perked up. "Yes, sir, no problem at all."

Jonathan stalked around the car, taking Eve's hand and pulling her through the enormous entryway into the lobby.

A man in his early twenties with a hipster beard smiled as they approached the registration desk. His little nametag read *Ethan*. "Good evening." He sounded far too cheerful for it to be real. "How can I help you today? Are you checking in?"

"That depends." Jonathan slid his driver's license and black AmEx card across the counter. "Are any of the villas available?"

Ethan's brows shot up. "You don't have a reservation, sir?"

"No. I'd prefer a villa, but a suite would be acceptable."

Picking up the two cards, Ethan glanced down at them before setting them next to his keyboard. "Just a moment, Mr. Hale," he said, grabbing the white mouse and clicking away at the large screen. "Let me see what we have available."

Jonathan brought Eve's hand up to his lips, kissing the backs of her knuckles. "Soon," he promised, sure the enormous hotel would be able to find something for them.

Sure enough, Ethan looked up with his over-the-top smile all of ten seconds later. "How long were you planning to stay with us?"

"Just tonight."

Relief filled the young man's eyes. "Excellent. The Signature Villa is available, but for tonight only. A large wedding party will be checking in tomorrow afternoon, taking all the villas."

It was the smallest of the three villas, if he remembered correctly. He hadn't stayed here in a while—not since he realized being a rich, hotshot CEO didn't make him too good to sleep at his parents' house when he visited. Everyone in the family had been relieved when he toned down the douchey behaviors a little bit.

"Sounds perfect," Jonathan said, not caring how big the space was, as long as they had as much privacy as possible.

Ethan typed and clicked away on his computer for a couple of minutes, then swiped the credit card. A printer farther down the counter spat out a receipt. "If you'll just sign here, Mr. Hale," he said, sliding the page, a pen, and both cards across the countertop.

Scrawling his signature on the line at the bottom, Jonathan handed back the pen and picked up his cards. He slid them into his wallet as the receptionist made two keys for their villa, slipping them into a little cardboard envelope with the hotel's logo on the front. Ethan grabbed a Sharpie next, using it to circle their villa on a map of the property, confirming that Jonathan remembered correctly.

"To get to your villa, you need to—"

"Thank you, but I've stayed there before," Jonathan interrupted, taking the keys and map from the counter. "I appreciate your help."

With Eve's hand still clasped in his, he went back outside, where the valet driver dutifully waited beside Lucy's Mercedes. He hoped to God this was the car his mom had used to pick them up from the airport, and his suitcase was still in the trunk. Eve told him the other day she'd brought it with them from Denver but forgot it in the car when they arrived at the house. It had only just occurred to him that he'd need some supplies to bring all the plans forming in his mind to fruition.

If not, he'd make do. He always did.

"Thank you," Jonathan said, handing the kid another fifty when he took the key back. He helped Eve into the passenger seat, closing her door for her, then slid back behind the wheel.

"You rented a whole villa just for us?" Eve asked, sounding bemused.

"With what I intend to do to you for the next several hours, trust me, you'll be glad we're not sharing walls with anyone else."

He glanced over in time to see her blush furiously in the light of the setting sun. Turning to look out the passenger side window didn't quite hide her small smile.

God, he hoped she was right—that she truly could trust him, and he wouldn't somehow fuck this all up. Because she was sure as fuck right about the rest of it. The caged energy sparking inside him would come out soon, one way or another. Better to release it in a controlled way, deeply pleasurable to them both, than to let it explode out of him on its own.

Jonathan pulled into one of the spots outside their villa. He put the car into park but left the engine running. "Before we go inside, we need to go over a few things."

Frowning up at him, she asked, "Like what?"

"Most importantly, I need to know you'll truly be okay."

"Jonathan—" she started, sounding impatient.

He held up a hand to stop her. "I know what you already said, and I heard you. But I just . . ." The sentence trailed off as he tried to figure out what to say.

Communication and honesty. With his dad's advice ringing in his mind, he knew exactly how to solve this issue.

"Early in their relationship, my parents did this thing to make sure they could always believe each other. They had a special code word, and if one of them said it, the other one had to be completely honest, no matter how hard it was." In that moment, he realized he never found out what their special word had been. He'd have to ask his mother soon.

The frustration left her eyes, and a smile tugged at her lips. "You want us to have a code word, too?"

Eve didn't merely understand his desire—she wanted this as much as he did. He could see it in her eyes. "I think it would help us both learn to trust each other in a way we haven't really trusted anyone else before."

Stretching across the center console, she pressed a warm, soft kiss against his lips. "I chose the safeword," she said, eyes bright as she pulled back. "Your turn."

He opened his mouth to answer, but nothing came out. "Huh," he said after several seconds. "This is harder than I thought. Now I feel bad for always making my subs choose."

Her answering laugh eased some of the pain and anger still roiling around inside him. "Try not to overthink it." She held up her hand, showing him her father's ring. "I just wrote down the first thing I saw."

"Okay, okay," he said. "The first thing I see. That makes our official code word *most beautiful woman in the world*."

A blush accompanied her dazzling grin, and he suddenly wanted to get this part over as quickly as possible. He ached to be inside her.

"I believe that would be a code phrase," she teased.

"True. And it's something that could easily come up in conversation, which would just be confusing."

Eve rolled her eyes, but her smile stayed firmly in place. "Whatever you say, prince charming."

Okay, if he didn't get on with things soon, he might end up hauling her over to the driver's seat and fucking her here in the parking lot. "Veritas," he said, remembering his Latin from his prep school days. "It means—"

"Truth," she finished for him. "I know. That's perfect."

"Good. Now that's settled, I have two questions for you. First, are you doing this only because you feel obligated to help me, but deep down you're terrified and wish you'd never offered?"

Before he even finished speaking, she started shaking her head. "No, that's not how I feel at all. I want this for you, but I also want it for me. You'll see just how much I want it when you take off my panties." The saucy little creature winked at him. "Veritas."

He didn't know whether to laugh or shove her dress out of the way and finger fuck her before they went inside. With a deep breath, he forced himself to carry on with his original plan. They needed to get inside for all his deviant plans to come to fruition. "Then here's my other question. Do you promise to use your safeword if things are too much for you?"

"Yes." Her answer was immediate. "Ver—"

"I know you, Eve," he interrupted. "I know you're going to want to keep going for my sake, no matter how you feel about it. So I need you to really think about this before you answer me."

She started to respond, but then closed her mouth, the corners dipping down into a small frown. At least half a minute passed before she spoke again. "You're right," she said, her earlier levity gone. "I would do that. I'd do anything to take some of this pain away from you."

"Truly hurting you would only make me feel worse," he told her. "I'm not willing to push you past your limits. Not ever. I need to be able to trust you to tell me where those limits are."

Eve nodded, understanding filling her eyes. "I promise to use my safeword if things go too far for me," she said, truth ringing in every word. "Veritas."

That would have to do. Killing the engine, he asked, "You ready?"

In answer, she scrambled out of the car, clearly as eager as him to get started. "California is so beautiful," she said, eyes bright as she turned in a full circle, taking everything in. "I've never seen anywhere else like this outside of movies."

"This is just southern California," he told her, slipping around the back of the car and popping the trunk. His cock twitched at the sight of the small black suitcase. When he reached for her hand again moments later, she threaded her fingers through his, holding him tight. "Northern California is a whole different place. We should drive up the coast sometime. Stop in all my favorite spots between here and Napa."

Warmth radiated from her eyes. "I'd love that."

So would he. Perhaps that was a trip they could plan sooner rather than later. It intrigued him, this idea of showing her the world he used to live in. Rediscovering his past with his present—and, if he was lucky, his future—by his side.

He led her into the villa, rolling the suitcase inside and dropping the car and room keys on the small table by the door.

"Holy shit, this place is incredible," she said in a muted, awe-filled voice, moving deeper inside as he locked the door. She passed the small kitchen and began exploring the living room, running her hands along the tops of the couch cushions as she eyed the enormous fireplace.

Grabbing his phone from his pocket, he pulled up the group chat with his mom, Maisie, and Alice. He typed up a quick message: *Eve and I are staying in a hotel for the night. We'll see you tomorrow.* Before any replies could come in, he turned the phone off, dropping it on the table next to the keys.

Eve had circled around the couch, and now stood beside a small wood table inlaid with a chessboard, the pieces already set and ready to play. She picked up the white queen, rolling the carved wooden piece between her fingers. "I can't believe this is r—"

Chess pieces scattered as Jonathan spun her around, pushing her into the table and molding his lips to hers. He ran his tongue along the seam of her lips, not so much requesting entrance as demanding it. The taste of sweet white wine overwhelmed his other senses when she relinquished control to him.

With a little whimpering moan, she arched her back, pressing her body flush against his. The heat of her felt so fucking good. But not enough. Nowhere fucking close.

A growl rose out of him as he twirled her back around, pushing forward until she had to place her hands flat on the chessboard to steady herself. "Sir, I—"

He silenced her with two swift spanks, one to either side of her ass. "Be still."

Eve didn't say another word as he rushed to undress her, his usual finesse and care flying out the window. The thin loop of thread attaching the tiny hook above the zipper snapped as he tried to undo it.

At least one seam popped as he yanked the partially unzipped dress off her shoulders and down over her hips.

Not caring in the least, he unhooked the clasp of the lacy black bra, managing not to damage this one. The panties didn't fare as well. He gripped them in one hand and yanked, a surge of excitement coursing through him as the sound of tearing fabric reached his ears. Her yelp only made his blood run hotter.

Pushing his hand firmly between her thighs, he cupped her pussy possessively, his thumb pressing against the tight ring of her asshole. He leaned down over her, hand squeezing. "You belong to me," he growled in her ear. "I'm going to use you tonight. That's what you want isn't it? To be used? To be my whipping post, my fucktoy? For me to take everything I'm feeling out on you?"

She whimpered again, and the sound somehow made his cock even harder. "Yes, Sir."

"Mmm," he murmured, biting down on the lobe of her ear hard enough for her to yelp again. "Be careful what you wish for."

Standing straight, he gathered her long, thick hair together, wrapping it tightly around his fist. When he yanked her upright, she let out a low hiss of pain. It was like music to his ears.

"Come," he ordered, leading her into the largest of the three bedrooms. He grinned when he saw they hadn't changed the furniture since the last time he stayed here. A king-sized, four poster bed dominated the space.

Perfect.

A red couch matching the one in the living room stood at the foot of the bed. He kicked it out of the way with so much force, it crashed into the desk nearby. Ignoring the useless furniture, he nudged Eve toward the foot of the bed. "Up," he ordered, pleasure pulsing in his chest as she scrambled onto the pristine white quilt.

She stopped in the middle of the bed to look back over her shoulder, a question in her eyes. Christ, she was beautiful, with her hair tumbling wildly over her shoulders, mouth parted slightly as she panted for air. Eve on her hands and knees, back arched, ass in the air, was one of the most captivating sights he'd ever seen.

Resisting the urge to climb up behind her and push into her wet heat, he got to work. First, he retrieved one of the pillows from the head of the bed, positioning it under her slim hips. With a hand at the small of her back, he pushed down until she lay nearly flat atop the mattress, only her ass elevated by the pillow.

For the next part, he had to get creative. Undoing his tie, he looped it around her wrist, making a knot just tight enough that she wouldn't be able to slip out. He attached the other end of the tie to the first bedpost.

"Stay," he ordered, moving back out into the living room in search of more ties. He checked the curtains by the French doors to their private patio first, but the cords holding them back were much too short.

Inspiration striking, he strode into one of the other bedrooms, throwing open the closet door. Jackpot. He pulled the terrycloth belts from the two robes. Swinging by the front door, he also retrieved his suitcase before returning to the master bedroom.

As far as he could tell, Eve hadn't moved a single muscle in his absence. "Good girl," he said, liking the way her cheeks flushed at the praise. He retrieved a third belt from the robes in their own closet, then got to work, tying her to the four posts.

When he finished, he stepped back to admire his work. She was now spread eagle, her arms and legs stretched out as far and straight as possible toward the four corners of the bed. Her tight rear hole and pussy were on glorious, lewd display, clearly visible between her pale cheeks.

"If the villas were all full, my plan was to gag you," he said, moving his bag to the now-crooked sofa and opening it. "Luckily, we don't have to worry about that here. You can scream as much as you want."

She buried her face in the quilt right before a muffled moan drifted out of her.

"Remind me of your safeword," Jonathan said as he made his selections from the bag. He remembered it, of course. But he needed her to remember that she could use it. Especially during a scene like this, when things would surely get extra intense.

Eve turned her head again, resting her cheek against the quilt. Her eyes found his across the room. "Emerald, Sir."

"Don't forget it." The first three items he needed in hand, he made his way to the side of the bed, laying them out on the mattress. "Now, let's get started."

Picking up a small bottle of lube, he removed the cap and upended it over the crack of her ass. The thick, viscous fluid cascaded down to her pussy and the pillow below.

The muscles of her ass flexed, as if she wanted to squeeze her cheeks together. But with her legs spread so wide, it was no longer possible.

"Relax," Jonathan ordered, smacking just below the curve of her right ass cheek. "It'll only hurt more if you don't."

She did as instructed for exactly three seconds. But then his finger plunged into her ass without warning, and every muscle in her body tensed. "Oh, God." She forced the words out between clenched teeth, squirming as much as her restraints would allow. "It *hurts*."

His chuckle came out a little crueler than he intended, low and rumbling and dark. "Trust me, Evie. My finger is the least of your worries right now."

She stilled. He'd never called her Evie before. For a moment, he thought she didn't like it, that she was about to object. But then her body relaxed, starting with her shoulders and rolling through the rest of her like a slow-moving wave.

"Good girl," he said again, pumping the single finger in and out of her a few times before adding a second. When he felt sure the lube coated her tight, inner walls, he removed his fingers and picked up a large, stainless-steel plug. In honor of her safeword, he'd packed one with an emerald-colored gem affixed to the end of the flared base.

He lowered the tip of the plug to her asshole, pushing gently against the tight ring of muscle. Eve's breaths came in harsh gasps as he spread her wider and wider, taking his time, wanting her to feel every inch of the plug as it entered her. When it finally settled into place, the gem on the base glinting in the lamplight, her whole body shook like a leaf.

On her application, she'd indicated that she had extensive experience with anal sex and rated all types and sizes of plugs as a five. Her reaction to the penetration both surprised and delighted him. "You don't actually like anal, do you?" he asked, lips spreading into an excited grin.

"No, Sir," she admitted, still trembling.

"But you'll do it anyway, because I do?" he pressed.

She took a deep, steadying breath, letting it out slowly through her nose. "It turns me on to do something I hate to make you happy."

Pulling the plug out just enough to make her gasp, he let go, letting it settle back into place. "Oh, you sweet girl," he said, bending to plant a soft kiss on her temple. "We're going to have so much fun together. Just remember your promise."

Jonathan backed away, finally shedding his jacket and draping it over the arm of the couch. His shirt followed close behind, and then he shed his shoes and socks, tossing them into a corner. Leaving his slacks on for now, he padded back over to the bed, his feet sinking into the plush rug.

Retrieving the final item he'd pulled from his bag, he wrapped his hand around the familiar, smooth handle. The paddle had seen so much use over the years that parts of the dark stain had rubbed away, revealing the blond wood beneath.

This paddle never entered the regular circulation of tools in the dungeon back home. It was the very first spanking implement he'd bought, older than the Manor itself. He and his college roommates—Leo, Aiden, and Mason—had long since waded into the shallow waters of BDSM, experimenting as best they could with belts and hands and flimsy, toy handcuffs when they could find a willing partner.

Jonathan was the first of them to dive into the deep end.

He swished the thick, rectangular paddle through the air once, refamiliarizing himself with its weight. Air whooshed through the five round holes spaced evenly down the center.

Even after all these years, the paddle remained his favorite instrument of punishment. Nothing else felt as perfect in his hand.

"I want you to count for me," he said as he moved into position.

"Yes, Sir."

Raising the paddle high above her, he brought it down across the center of her ass, only hard enough to sting. Eve's eyes screwed shut and her hands balled into fists, but she didn't make a sound. After a few seconds, she whispered, "One."

"Good girl." He brought the paddle down on her ass again, a little harder this time.

Air hissed out of her like a leaking tire. "Two."

They made it all the way to ten before he decided she'd had enough of a warmup. Her ass was a uniform rosy pink, and when he brushed his hand over the skin, it was warm to the touch.

Closing his eyes, Jonathan let all the pain and anger and fear and frustration of the last week course through him. He made himself breathe through the chaos of emotions, funneling it all toward the one thing that could calm them.

Eve.

She guided him through the worst storm of his life and brought him out mostly whole on the other side.

Here she was, doing it all over again. Offering her body and her submission to him—a safe place to weather another storm.

He would get through this. He could get through anything so long as he didn't lose her too.

Opening his eyes, he brought down the paddle on the downward curve of her ass, using enough force this time that she couldn't hold in a startled scream.

Eve struggled to catch her breath for several seconds, her face buried in the quilt to hide her tears. When at last her shoulders moved up and down with a near-steady rhythm, she gave him a muffled, "Eleven."

Before she could brace herself, he delivered the next stroke to the same exact place.

Expecting it this time, she used the quilt to dull the sound of her scream, forcing out, "Twelve," long before he expected it. Her voice shook with the effort.

Jonathan cupped a hand under her chin, turning her face toward him. "Don't hide from me," he told her, taking in her splotchy skin and red, puffy eyes. His breath caught in his throat at the sight. She was just so fucking perfect.

Some women cried demurely. Some prettily. Eve cried with her entire fucking body, and it was such a beautiful thing to witness. He wanted to see every tear, hear every gasp and scream and ragged breath. He wanted her to give him everything.

Her head jerked when he brought down the paddle again, but she stopped herself at the last second, settling back into the position he'd requested. He got to watch her face as the pain exploded through her—got to see each and every minute change as she settled into it.

"Thirteen."

"Fuck," he muttered, gripping his cock through his slacks. He squeezed hard enough for it to hurt, desperate to take the worst of the edge off. Combined with the riot of emotions still coursing through him, he found it nearly impossible to focus on anything but his desire to bury his cock inside of her.

You're a fucking professional, damnit, he bellowed in his mind. *Get a fucking grip.*

The worst of it faded, leaving behind a dull throb of pleasure that no longer threatened to overwhelm him. "It's time to accelerate things," he told her, moving back in position at the side of the bed. "As long as you still want to continue."

"I do. Veritas."

Relief surged through him. "There will be no need to count anymore."

As the words, "Yes, Sir," passed through her quivering lips, he landed the hardest stroke of all. He didn't even wait for her scream to end before he did it again.

Again.

Again.

Everything about her was perfect. The way her ass cheeks rose with the force of each blow before settling back into place. The tears streaming down her face as she sobbed. The rasp in her screams as her throat got sore.

But most of all, the way she didn't thrash or pull at her bonds. Not even once.

She was entirely his, giving over every inch of her body, every corner of her mind. It was an offering he would never take for granted.

The paddle fell to the rug with a dull *thud*. Moving to the foot of the bed, he undid the ties around the two posts rising out of the footboard, freeing her legs. He shed his slacks and boxer briefs as quickly as he could, flinging them in the general direction of his shoes.

He needed to be inside her. He needed it right fucking now.

Not bothering to undo the knots around her ankles, he climbed into the bed between her legs, forcing her up onto her knees. The restraints on her wrists kept her head and upper torso flat against the mattress, arms still spread wide.

Jonathan pressed his hands against the scalding hot flesh of her ass, digging his fingers in just so he could hear her groan. Her skin had turned a deep, glorious crimson.

The poor thing wouldn't be able to sit for a week.

He grinned as he pulled the plug free, dropping it onto the bed and retrieving the bottle of lube. "Are you ready for me to fuck your ass?"

She only whimpered in response.

As soon as he coated his cock in a layer of lube, he pushed the head against her tightest opening. "Relax for me," he said, gripping her hips with both hands, spreading her ass wide with his thumbs. "Be a good girl."

Eve let out a strangled cry when he finally pushed past the tight ring. "It hurts," she said again, clenching her jaw against the pain.

Inching his way deeper, he took his time, letting her get used to him. By the time his pelvis pressed gently against her ass, she had finally started to untense.

"I want you to ask me to fuck you." She immediately started to answer, but he didn't give her the chance yet. "To be clear, this isn't an order. You get to choose. If you don't want this, but are willing to suffer it anyway, don't say a word. If you want me to fuck your pussy instead, say your safeword. I'll never make you do something against your will. But if you want this pain—if you *want* to give this to me—ask for it."

She clenched so tight around him, he barely managed to hold back a moan. Even from his position behind her, he could see that her pupils dilated as he spoke. "Please fuck my ass, Sir," she said, voice trembling with need. "I want to be exactly what you need. I want to submit to you in every way, no matter how much it hurts." She squeezed her muscles around his cock again, this time on purpose. "Please let me give you this."

Jonathan pulled most of the way out of her, and then slammed back in with so much force that she moved an inch up the bed. Her scream sounded different this time—equal parts pain and pleasure. And it drove him fucking wild.

Digging his fingers even deeper into her hips and ass, he settled into a fast rhythm, pulling her back against his cock each time he slammed forward. The only sounds in the room were her continued cries, the rough pants of his breath, and the sound of skin slapping against skin.

So. Fucking. Good.

He pounded into her like a man possessed, losing himself in physical sensation, finally escaping the turmoil of his mind. When he started getting close, he lifted one leg, planting his foot on the mattress to give him extra leverage. Grabbing a fistful of her hair to hold her in place, he slipped the middle finger of his other hand into his mouth, swirling his tongue once around the digit.

When he pressed the tip of the saliva-covered finger against her clit, her whole body bucked. "That's it," he said, matching the rhythm of his finger to that of his hips. "Come for me, Evie. I want to know what it feels like to be inside your ass when you come."

He pressed harder, fucked harder—forcing her closer and closer to the edge whether she wanted it or not. When at last she fell, she clenched so tight around him that he toppled over right after her, his whole body spasming as he came.

Jesus fucking Christ, he'd never fucked anything this tight in his entire life. He screwed his eyes shut as they bucked and shuddered together, riding out the storm trying to rip them apart from the inside out.

Her voice broke on her final scream, low and raspy and utterly spent. It amazed him she could still make any sound at all.

Eve's whole body trembled as he carefully pulled out of her, the muscles in her legs clearly on the verge of giving out. Helping her settle down against the mattress, he leaned over her tiny, perfect body so he could untie the knots at her wrists.

As soon as he got her free, he settled down beside her, pulling her tight against his chest. Her breaths still came in gasps as she molded her body to his, pressing against him from head to toe. Jonathan stroked her hair as her breathing slowly returned to normal.

"Thank you, Evie." He whispered it into her ear right before she fell asleep in his arms.

CHAPTER 16

Eve

No one questioned why they'd stayed at a hotel, which was a major relief. *That* wasn't something she wanted to try explaining to anyone, least of all his mother.

Jonathan and Eve walked into the house the next morning to find breakfast in full swing, the dining room table laden with stacks of pancakes, a platter full of bacon and sausage, and what looked like an enormous crystal punch bowl full of scrambled eggs. People called out or waved in greeting as they took seats at the table, and that was that.

After everyone stuffed themselves, Eve worked with Jonathan's brothers-in-law to do all the washing up, while the others stayed in the dining room. Lucy sat at the head of the table, Jonathan and Maisie to her right, and Alice to her left, while they made a list of all the things they still needed to do to settle Orson's estate.

Not wanting to intrude, Eve had gone into the living room with Sean and Dillon after they'd cleaned the kitchen. Barely five minutes passed before Jonathan texted her, asking if she'd be willing to sit in the dining room instead. He promised it was okay to decline, even including *veritas* in the message so she'd be sure to believe him.

The request surprised her, but if it made him happy, she couldn't see any harm.

Other than to her ass. The fancy, high-backed dining room chairs didn't even have cushions. She made the best of it, squirming as discreetly as she could to relieve the ache in her well-punished bottom.

Within minutes, it became abundantly clear that they didn't need or even want her help. Jonathan just wanted her near for some reason. Leaving them to their work, she read a book on her phone, trying to be as quiet and unobtrusive as possible.

Papers covered much of the long mahogany table now, organized into over a dozen short stacks. Other than the occasional bathroom break, none of them had left the room for hours.

"Okay," Jonathan said, finally leaning back to scan the list they'd compiled. "I'll take care of all this in the next few days. You don't need to worry about a thing."

The three women all looked at each other, eyebrows raised.

Jonathan eyed them suspiciously. "What's that look supposed to mean?"

The look between his mom and sisters turned from knowing to uncomfortable in an instant. Eve put her phone down to watch whatever the hell this was, a string of half-formed theories whirring through her mind.

It was Lucy who finally met Jonathan's gaze, reaching across the table to put her hand over his. She'd clearly been chosen as their designated spokesperson. "Sweetheart, we all talked last night after the funeral. We think you should head home."

Oh, shit. That hadn't even been on her list of possibilities. She watched her boyfriend's face like a hawk, knowing he wouldn't take this well at all.

But the anger and frustration she expected never materialized. Their scene last night must have done him even more good than she thought.

Jonathan stared at his mother in silence for several seconds, not moving a muscle. He didn't even blink. "Why?" he finally managed to ask. "Did I do something wrong? Is this because I punched Warren?"

"No," Lucy assured him, shaking her head. "Frankly, I'm glad you broke that son of a bitch's nose. He's had it coming for a long time."

One corner of Jonathan's lips twitched, though a bewildered sort of sadness still lingered in his eyes. "Then why don't you want me here?"

"It's not that we don't want you here, sweetheart." The love written all over Lucy's face made that abundantly clear. "We just don't *need* you here."

Jonathan's brows pulled together, forming a deep V. "What does that even mean?"

"All the hardest parts are done," Lucy said. "The people who live here can easily handle the rest. Your life is three thousand miles away."

When Jonathan started to object, Maisie bumped her shoulder against his. "We all know you like to be in charge," she joked, and Eve had to repress a snort. Talk about an understatement. "But we've got this part. Seriously."

Reaching across the table, Alice gently pulled the list free from Jonathan's fingers. He resisted at first, but then let go with a deep sigh.

"I see the decision has already been made," he said in a strangely monotone way, staring down at his now empty hand. His expression completely closed off, he pushed his chair back, stood, and buttoned his jacket. "If you'll excuse me." Shoulders stiff, he strode from the room.

Indecision erupted inside of Eve, an edge of panic speeding up her heartbeat. He hadn't asked her to go with him. Should she follow or give him some space? She had absolutely no idea what he'd want right now.

He'd just passed from the dining room to the foyer when Lucy called out, "He loved you, Jonathan. He loved you so goddamn much."

Eve held her breath as Jonathan froze. His hands curled into tight fists before slowly unfurling, like a flower spreading its petals toward the sun.

A single tear slipped down Lucy's wrinkled cheek as she stood, moving toward her son with tentative steps. "He was so proud of you when you founded HSS. He used to send press releases about your company to all his friends. But you know what made him even prouder?"

A strangled sound came out of him, as if he'd tried and failed to speak. After a moment of silence, he shook his head.

"When you sold HSS and started the Manor."

Jonathan whirled around, his dark eyes bright with tears. "There's no way that's true."

With a solemn nod, Lucy said, "He knew you were doing what you truly loved. It's so obvious how much happier you are now. We can all see it."

"It's true," Maisie said, her voice shaking. All of them were crying now. "You've been a whole different person since you started the Manor. Dad used to talk about it all the time."

A pair of tears started a slow descent down Jonathan's cheeks. "I wish I talked to him more. That I took more time off to visit. But it's too late."

"Oh, sweetheart." Lucy cupped his cheek with her hand. "I promise you, he never felt ignored or forgotten. Do you have any idea how happy he was when you called him last week? How proud he was that you came to him for advice? I don't think I've seen a bigger smile on that man's face since Maisie's wedding last year."

The muscles in his jaw clenched as he tried to regain control. "Really?"

"He was happy when he died," Lucy said, her voice breaking on the final word. "I can't tell you how grateful I am for that."

Jonathan lost the last vestiges of his tenuous control, his face crumpling as he started to cry in earnest. Gathering him into her arms, Lucy held him close, whispering about how proud they both were as he sobbed.

When Alice held out a box of tissues, Eve and Maisie both took several. Eve swiped at her eyes and tried to breathe through her torrent of tears. Her heart ached, and she longed to go to him. To wrap him in her warm embrace until he knew, without any room left for doubt, how truly wonderful he was. But she knew that would have to wait—this moment was for his family.

She had no idea how long they all cried. It could've been one minute or ten. All she knew was that the tension Jonathan had carried in his shoulders for the last several days had finally disappeared.

"What was the word?" Jonathan asked, his voice barely a whisper. "The one you two said so you always knew you could trust each other."

When Lucy smiled, she looked years younger. It lit up her entire face. "Edamame," she said with a little laugh.

Jonathan pulled away, eyebrows arched high. "You've got to be joking."

"We were at this little sushi place in LA when Orson came up with the idea," she said, her smile growing even wider. "We were eating edamame, and I guess we weren't feeling creative at the time. Sorry if that's not as profound or romantic as you hoped."

He stared at his mother for several seconds, shock still written all over his face. And then he burst out laughing. "I should've known. You two never took anything seriously in your lives."

"Not if we could help it," Lucy agreed, eyes still crinkling at the corners.

Sighing, Jonathan wiped the wetness away from his cheeks. "All right. I guess I'd better go pack."

Alice stood and hurried over to him, putting a hand on his arm. "We're not forcing you to leave or anything. If it helps you to be here, stay as long as you want."

"We just know how busy you always are," Maisie added, her frown remarkably similar to her brother's. "We were afraid you'd feel like you had to stay and be in charge of everything, like you always do. When really you'd rather be back at the Manor, spanking ass and taking names."

Another startled laugh bubbled out of him. "I can't believe you just said that."

"Not gonna lie," Maisie said with a little smirk, "I've had that one in my back pocket for a while now. I've just been waiting for the perfect opportunity to use it."

Eve had no trouble seeing why he'd always been extra close to his baby sister. The woman was a goddamn delight.

"You guys are right," Jonathan said once silence fell over the room again. "I know you are." With a smile that didn't quite reach his eyes, he looked over at Eve. "We'll leave first thing tomorrow morning."

The plane ride home was much more subdued than the trip out to

Denver. The air of mystery and excitement had been engulfed by sorrow and a deep, permeating exhaustion.

Eve slipped in and out of consciousness as the jet traversed the country, while Jonathan stared at his laptop, not even pretending to get any work done. His screen showed the same page of the same document every time she looked.

"Are you doing okay?" she finally asked when he started aimlessly scrolling between the pages, far too fast to read anything.

Abandoning the ruse, he shut his laptop and put it on one of the empty seats. He patted a hand on his lap, and she settled sideways over his thighs without hesitation, leaning into his chest and tucking her head under his chin. Her legs stretched out onto her old seat.

Jonathan sighed as he wrapped his arms around her, enveloping her with his warmth. "I know what I need to do," he said, sounding wearier than she'd ever heard him. "Go home, take clients, finish the expansion, keep living my life. But I—I don't know." He sighed again. "I just don't *want* to. Which sounds even whinier out loud than it did in my head."

"It doesn't sound whiny at all," she assured him, smiling at his sardonic tone. "No one would want to go back to regularly scheduled programming after the week you've had. If you did, I'd be kind of worried, actually."

He grunted noncommittally.

Chewing on her bottom lip, Eve tried to figure out how to help. "I know for a fact no one at the Manor expects you to take any clients for a while."

"How do you know that?" A new sharpness entered his tone.

"No one was gossiping behind your back," she said, knowing exactly where his mind went. "At the luncheon, when you went for that walk, Zach said he didn't think he'd be able to do the kind of work you all do right after losing a parent, and the rest of them agreed. I promise that was it."

He relaxed slightly beneath her. "I suppose it's for the best. God only knows what I'd do to them in this state of mind."

Squirming over his hard thighs, Eve quipped, "God and me, you mean."

That finally brought a small chuckle out of him, and the tension left his muscles completely. "I suppose the rest of it won't be so bad." He didn't sound like he believed it.

"I'll take as much off your plate for the expansion as I can," she promised, wanting to remove as much of his stress as possible. "I suspect your partners will, too. Just keep reminding yourself—you're not alone. Not by a long shot."

"I'll try." He didn't sound particularly confident, but she believed he would do his best not to forget.

It would have to do for now.

Not long after that, Jonathan drifted off to sleep, his arms dropping to his sides. For a second, she considered the best way to extricate herself from his lap without waking him. But in the end, she decided it would be better to stay put. The man had hardly slept since that first night in California, so she knew how desperately he needed this rest.

With her ear against his chest, she listened to the slow, rhythmic beating of his heart, closing her eyes, letting it surround her. The longer she listened, the more it soothed her worries and fears away. Though the effect was only temporary, she made up her mind to enjoy it as long as she could.

Jonathan didn't wake until they started their descent into Burlington. By then, her back and hips ached from staying in that position for so long, but she didn't mind. The plane landed smoothly, and only a few minutes passed before they arrived at their gate.

They had a lot more luggage now than they did on the flight out of Vermont. For one thing, Jonathan had a garment bag stuffed full of the suits Zach mailed. She also had a bag now—a small rolling suitcase she bought on clearance, filled with the clothes she had no choice but to buy in California. While Jonathan kept a good part of his wardrobe at the Manor for when he spent the night with a guest, Zach had no way of getting into her hotel room to access her clothes.

Oh, well. At least most of it had been on sale. And really, she needed to expand her new wardrobe far more than her initial foray into shopping after she dumped Frank. That had only been enough to get her by while she figured out her new life. Since a permanent position at Cox Construction was all but assured at this point, she figured what the hell.

Angelica, the auburn-haired driver, waited for them directly across from the doors when they stepped outside. As far as Eve could tell, she had on the exact same suit as the first time they met. "Welcome back, Mr. Hale, Ms. Hutchinson," she said in an over-the-top cheerful voice. She rushed over to relieve them of the luggage. "I hope you enjoyed your trip?"

Clearly, she didn't know why they'd extended it by almost a week. Jonathan had gone very still beside her, so she hurried to answer, "Thank you. We're glad to be home."

If her non-answer seemed off, Angelica did nothing to show it. "Tank is full, and keys are in the ignition," she said as she stowed the luggage in the trunk.

Wordlessly, Jonathan handed her a bunch of bills and climbed behind the wheel, shutting the door a little too hard.

The driver frowned—at least until she glanced down and saw how much easy cash she'd just made. "Is there anything else I can do for you?" she asked, that almost too-wide smile of hers firmly back in place.

"No. Thank you for everything." Eve gave the woman a smile she hoped didn't look too strained and got into the car.

Jonathan sighed as soon as she shut her door. "That was rude. She has no idea about my dad. I shouldn't have reacted like that."

"Well, you must have paid her extra well," she said, nudging him with her shoulder. "As soon as she looked at what you gave her, she very much didn't care."

He grunted in response—only the second time he'd done that to her since they met. Frowning, she decided not to say anything about it. At least not yet. He deserved a hell of a lot of leeway as he discovered his path through the murky landscape of grief.

Eve would help him as much as she could, but she knew no two paths were quite the same. For so much of it, he'd have to figure things out on his own.

It fucking sucked.

Most of the drive passed in silence, Jonathan staring intently at the road, hands far too tight on the steering wheel. Eve wracked her brain for something to say to pull him out of his gloom, or to at least distract him for a while. But every single idea she came up with sounded idiotic.

The sun was creeping toward the horizon when at last she started to recognize where they were. They'd arrive back at the Manor in about twenty minutes or so.

Relief coursed through her. As much as she wanted to be there for Jonathan, the uneasy silence had her on edge. Not to mention the pain still lingering in her lower back from staying in that weird position for so long on the plane. A tension headache had only just begun pulsing across her forehead and at the base of her skull.

Eve dug through her purse until she found her keys, buried all the way at the bottom. They jangled together as she pulled them out, and she wrapped her fist around them to stop the noise.

For the first time in over an hour, Jonathan looked in her direction. Gaze zeroing in on her clenched hand, he frowned. "You won't be needing those tonight." He had his eyes back on the road before he even finished speaking.

The matter-of-fact way he said it surprised her so much, it took her several seconds to respond. "I'd like you to drop me off at my car, please." She kept her voice even and inflectionless, not wanting him to think she was upset. Even though she kind of was . . . but the last thing she wanted right now was for him to get defensive. That never helped any situation.

He let out a loud breath—something between a sigh and an annoyed huff. "I'd appreciate your cooperation on this." Despite that weird sound he made, his voice held no hint of frustration. In fact, he sounded far too infuriatingly reasonable considering he was disregarding her preferences entirely. "I'm tired and I don't want to drive out of my way. And to be honest, I just don't think I can be alone right now."

The vulnerability in that last sentence made her heart ache, and she fucking hated it. Of course he'd feel vulnerable right now. Of course he'd want her there. It was the most reasonable thing in the world.

Thus making her a giant fucking asshole if she dared object again. It was as if, in this moment, her own needs didn't matter at all. Which was a shitty fucking feeling. Especially after she'd put his needs above hers every moment of the last week.

"I understand," she forced herself to say. At least none of her frustration came through into her voice. "Of course I'll stay with you. I only wanted to go to my hotel because I'm really tired too. I planned to go straight to bed."

"Don't worry," Jonathan said, his grip on the steering wheel finally loosening. He had to have some horrific hand cramps by now. "We can go right to bed. Your body needs a long rest after that last scene anyway."

Holding in a sigh, Eve stared out the window as they drove past the exit that would lead to Fairford without even slowing down.

CHAPTER 17

Jonathan

He may have fucked up a little bit.

Guilt sat heavy in his chest, weighing him down all day. It wasn't a feeling he cared for, and usually he'd seek out the injured party, apologize or make amends as necessary, and get on with his life.

Only problem was, he had no idea what he did.

All he knew was that he'd come to rely on Eve this last week. Whenever his grief started overwhelming him, he let her warmth seep into him, enveloping his heart like a protective shell.

When he woke up this morning and found Eve sitting cross-legged on his bed, leaning back against his headboard, he could tell instantly that the temperature had dropped several degrees. The sudden change confused him so much, he couldn't build up the nerve to ask about it.

Even now, almost twelve hours later, he balked at the idea of bringing it up. What was he supposed to say? *Hey, you seem to be mad, but I have no idea why. Can we please talk about it so I can understand?*

Jonathan was halfway through that last thought before he realized it didn't sound as absurd as he expected. In fact, it seemed a hell of a lot more mature than hiding in his office all day, hoping she didn't need him to sign anything until he figured it out on his own.

None of his past relationships with women had prepared him for this. Perhaps because none of them had ever been real relationships.

With a sigh, he went over to the antique, glass-fronted bookcase he used as his private liquor cabinet and turned the old skeleton key. Opening one of the doors, he grabbed the most expensive bottle he had in there. He pulled out the fleur-de-lis shaped glass stopper, poured a single mouthful into a small tulip glass, and tipped it into his mouth.

The Louis XIII cognac was far too precious to knock back like a standard drink. He let the liquid linger on his tongue, closing his eyes and focusing on the subtle flavors. First honey and figs. Then plum, leather, smoke, and more he couldn't name.

Only when his mind had completely calmed did he finally swallow. The liquor went down smooth, leaving behind the most exquisite burn.

"Okay," he said out loud, returning the hand-blown glass decanter to the cabinet and locking it. "Time to act like a fucking adult."

Jonathan took his time descending to the first floor and out through the back of the house. That single swallow had calmed his racing thoughts, dulling the urgency of his confusion and unease. He would find her, calmly ask for a private talk, and get to the bottom of this before anything got out of hand. Simple as that.

Eve's scream pierced through the quiet evening, so loud that even the forest noises halted for a moment.

Heartbeat kicking back up into high gear, he sprinted toward the new building, dirt and gravel kicking up behind him as he crossed the unpaved courtyard. "Eve?" he shouted as soon as he burst through the front doors. "Where are you?"

She didn't answer, but she didn't really need to. Not with the cacophony of noise coming from upstairs.

Taking the stairs two at a time, he followed the commotion into one of the new almost-finished suites. Just as he passed through the doorless frame, part of a floor tile flew through the bathroom doorway, skidding to a stop near the windows.

What in the *fuck*.

"Eve?" he called again, crossing over to the bathroom in four long strides. "What are you—" The question trailed off as his mouth dropped open.

Not even seeming to notice him, Eve slammed a hammer down against one of the recently laid floor tiles. Dust billowed up from the floor as sharp pieces of tile flew everywhere. Eve gathered up the fragments in her bare hands, flinging them aside. Broken, ruined tiles surrounded her in every direction, making the room look like a bomb went off.

"Evie, what's going on?" Shock made his voice so low, she might not have even heard him.

A sob burst out of her as she picked up a crowbar with trembling hands. Wedging it between the tile's backer board and the subfloor, she pried the underside of the tile off in one large piece. As soon as it popped loose, she grabbed it without any care, slicing the palm of her hand open on a sharp edge. Ignoring the gash, she peered at the bottom of the backer board, running her fingers over the remains of the mortar, then doing the same to the now-exposed subfloor.

"Goddamnit!" she shouted, tears making muddy tracks in the dust clinging to her face. Dropping the crowbar with a loud *clang*, she reached for the hammer again, not even seeming to notice the blood now dripping down her wrist.

It was the blood that finally snapped him out of his stupor. Tile bits crunched under his shoes as he hurried to the center of the destroyed room, grabbing Eve's wrist before she could slam the hammer down.

She shrieked and toppled away from him, landing in a graveyard of jagged shards. Another scream barreled out of her as the sharp points dug into her skin.

"Evie!" He shouted this time, needing her to hear him. "It's me, it's okay." Scooping her up off the floor, he tried to pull her into a tight embrace, wanting to calm and soothe her as quickly as possible.

Wriggling out of his grip before he got a proper hold on her, she dropped back to her knees. Her frantic eyes searched the floor until she found the hammer.

Before she could snatch up the bloody tool, Jonathan grabbed her again. This time, he made sure to do so in a way that she wouldn't be able to get away from him.

"No!" She struggled and kicked as he hauled her out of the bathroom. "Let go! Let me go back!" When she started fighting even harder, he had no choice but to twist her around and fling her over his shoulder.

"Jonathan!" She shouted his name over and over as she banged her fists against his back, legs still kicking furiously.

He ignored her protests and attacks, easily keeping his hold on her as he carried her downstairs and outside. His hope was that the fresh air and soft, evening light would snap her out of it, but no luck. As she continued to thrash and scream like a trapped wildcat, a new idea popped into his head.

Striding through the garden, he opened the gate at the far end with his free hand, hurrying through it. And then he dumped her unceremoniously into the pool.

Jonathan watched her with unblinking eyes, ready to jump in the moment it looked like she needed his help. But she burst to the surface after only a few seconds, spluttering and wiping water from her eyes.

"What the fuck, Jonathan?" she demanded, half indignant, half bewildered.

Squatting down, he waited until she kicked her way over to the side. Grabbing both her wrists, he easily hauled her up onto the pool deck. "Better?" he asked, pushing her dripping hair back from her face.

"Fuck off." Determination in every line of her face, she started back toward the gate.

Jonathan hurried after her, easily catching up with his much longer legs. "You're not going back in there until you talk to me."

"Watch me," she threw over her shoulder.

Grabbing her around the waist, he hauled her to the nearest pool chaise. Sitting on the edge of the cushion, he forced Eve down over his lap.

"Let go of me!" she shouted, but he ignored her.

Trapping her kicking legs between his, he started to spank. He knew her wet jeans would dull away most of the pain, but he didn't care. This wasn't about punishment. He just needed to do something —anything—to help her calm down and start thinking rationally again.

A long stream of insults and expletives flowed out of her, but he ignored them. Holding her in place with the vise of his legs and a hand pressed firmly against the small of her back, he kept spanking in a perfect rhythm, never letting up for even a second.

It took far longer than he expected for the fight to seep out of her. His hand hurt like a motherfucker by the time she finally drooped over his thigh, spent and boneless.

"Okay, you can let me up now," she said, sounding utterly defeated. "Please."

Releasing her trapped legs, he helped her into position on his lap, holding her close to his chest. Still dripping wet, she shivered in the late spring air. "Tell me what happened," he said, soft and encouraging.

Without a word, Eve held up her right hand. The heavy gold ring still sat on her middle finger, a gaping hole where the large, square cut emerald used to be.

He stared at it, uncomprehending, for a few seconds. Then the whole messy situation made sense in an instant.

"You tiled that bathroom this morning," he said.

"Yes. I have no idea when it fell out. Or even *how* it fell out." She made a miserable little noise, almost sounding like a wounded animal. "I don't know what to do."

With gentle fingers, he pulled her hand up toward his face, examining the ring. It only took a moment for him to figure out the issue. The bezel around three of the sides had worn away to almost nothing with time.

It clearly hadn't been a question of if the gem would fall out. Only a matter of when.

She started crying by the time he finished explaining what happened. "I didn't even know that could happen," she said, sniffling.

"It's going to be okay," he promised. "I'll help you find it."

"Wanna know the worst part of all this?" she asked, swiping her nose with the back of her hand. "I hate this stupid thing." She held her hand out again so they could examine the piece of jewelry. "It's big and clunky and ugly. Way too heavy. And I fucking hate yellow gold."

He almost asked why she still wore it then, but realized he already knew the answer. "But you're afraid to take it off," he said gently. "For the same reason you didn't want to stop working at your dad's company. It feels like letting go of him."

"Frank made me get rid of the rest of my dad's things," she told him in a small voice. "This is all I have left."

"I'm so sorry," he said, taking her hand in his. "I'll make sure—"

He stopped when he saw her wince.

Frowning, he flipped her hand over. The deep cut across her palm still oozed blood at a sluggish pace. Smaller nicks and gouges marred her fingers and forearm. "Christ, look at you," he said, the tight, twisting pain of fear blooming in his chest. "I'm taking you to the ER."

Eve yanked her hand out of his, leaning back so she could peer into his face. "That's a bit much, don't you think?" she asked, frowning. "Just give me a first aid kit. I'll be fine."

But he was already standing, pulling her up with him. "This isn't up for debate," he said, leading her through the garden with an arm around her shoulders. "Let's both get into some dry clothes, and then we're going."

"Jonathan, come on," she said, exasperation saturating the words. "I'm fine."

He didn't even dignify that with a response.

"For fuck's sake," she muttered under her breath, not fighting as he steered her toward the main house.

CHAPTER 18

Eve

Frustration still roiled inside Eve as she hurried through the new building the next morning. It wouldn't take much more for it to start boiling over.

Jonathan's heavy handedness last night had made her want to scream. Not only did he drag her two towns over to the nearest hospital, where—*shocker*—all they did was clean and bandage the various wounds. But then he insisted she sleep at his house, once again refusing to drive her back to her car.

"Why?" she demanded when he had announced his intentions, crossing her arms and glaring at him.

Keeping his eyes on the road, he'd said, "You're hurt. I want to keep an eye on you—make sure you're okay." As if she just had surgery and needed a temporary caretaker.

"Jonathan—" she started.

"I know you want to keep looking for the emerald," he'd interrupted, finally glancing her way. The hint of an apology lurked deep in his eyes. "But it'll have to wait. Everything will be exactly as you left it tomorrow."

Only that wasn't true. She skidded to a stop halfway down the upstairs corridor, eyes going wide. Of the twenty suites on this floor, only one of them had a door.

The one she'd worked on yesterday.

Something that sounded startlingly like a growl came out of her as she ran the rest of the way to the door. There was no point in trying the handle, but she did it anyway.

Locked. Of course it was locked.

Her hands balled into fists. The dozens of tiny injuries all stung, and a stab of genuine pain emanated from the larger cut on her palm. Ignoring the discomfort, she went right back downstairs, stalking into the enormous ballroom that made up most of the first floor.

Perched atop a sixteen-foot ladder, Lainey worked on the wiring for one of the enormous Venetian glass chandeliers. Two of her stronger employees stood on either side of an adjacent ladder, holding the custom-made light fixture half a foot below the ceiling while their boss worked.

"Lainey," she started, unable to keep the fury out of her voice.

"Not a good time," the other woman answered in a distracted tone.

Undeterred, Eve said, "Why is there a door on room 206?"

Lainey's hands stilled, and after a moment, she sighed. "Mr. Hale texted me last night. He asked me to have some workers come in early to install the door and lock before you got here."

An icy cold spread through her, starting in the center of her chest.

How. Fucking. Dare he.

"Give me the key," she demanded.

"I don't have one." Lainey fidgeted with the wire stripper on the top platform of the ladder. "He told me to only make one copy and put it in his office."

"Goddamnit, Lainey!" Eve shouted, so loud that the two men on the second ladder jumped, almost dropping the absurdly expensive chandelier. "This is bullshit, and you know it!"

Looking down at her for the first time since she entered the room, Lainey at least had the good grace to appear remorseful. "I'm sorry, Eve. He explained what happened, and I know how much you want to get in there. But he owns the damn building. I didn't have a choice."

With a disgusted sound, Eve whirled around and hurried from the room, heading straight through the front doors and outside. As she stormed through the garden, she looked up at the third-floor window of Jonathan's office. It didn't surprise her in the least to find him standing there, looking down at her with no expression on his face.

Eyes narrowing, she ran the rest of the way into the house, sprinting straight past a startled Remy, who called out after her. Ignoring him, she went through the house as fast as her legs could carry her, bursting through the office door without knocking. "Give me the fucking key," she demanded between gasping breaths.

By now, Jonathan sat rigid behind his desk, hands folded placidly on the desktop in front of him. "Why don't you sit down," he said, voice as devoid of emotion as his face.

Not moving from her spot by the door, Eve took several moments to get her breathing back under control. In a low, dangerously calm voice, she said again, "Give me. The fucking. Key."

With a soft, almost inaudible sigh, Jonathan stood and walked around the side of the desk. "I'm doing this for your own good," he said once he stood a few feet in front of her.

"You don't get to decide what's for my own good," she spat. "Only I get to do that."

Frustration flashed in his eyes, but he repressed it immediately. "I'm not being unreasonable here, and deep down, I think you know that. You're hurt, Evie. Wait until you've healed, and then you can destroy that bathroom to your heart's content. Just make sure you wear protective gear next time."

Eve wanted to start yelling. To pound her fists against his chest. To call him every horrible name she could think of and, unlike last night, actually mean every word of it.

Breathing slowly through her nose, she counted in her head until the most violent of those desires subsided. She made it all the way to a hundred and fifteen.

"If you had talked to me about this, maybe I would've been okay with it." Probably not, but she may have gone along with it anyway just to appease him. "But you pulled this shit behind my back. That's fucked up, Jonathan. That's *really* fucked up."

"You're hurt," he said again, as if that excused everything. "I—"

"I have a few cuts," she said, flinging her bandaged hands up in the air. "The nurse said I didn't even need to be there. Don't pretend you didn't hear him."

Jonathan didn't answer, his face as stony and unreadable as ever.

"I freaked out last night when I realized the emerald was missing," she said. "I admit it. But I'm *fine*. Give me the key and let me get back to work."

Pity entered his dark eyes then. Fucking pity. "I know this is important to you, but it's not worth injuring yourself even m—"

"You don't understand," Eve interrupted.

His lips compressed into a tight, angry line. "Of course I understand. Or did you forget that my father died last week."

"Oh, it must have slipped my mind," she shot back, laying on the sarcasm as thick as she could. "How silly of me."

Lips thinning even more, he took several seconds to compose himself before responding. "Be careful. You're on very thin ice right now."

"Oh, fuck off," she said, glaring. "You still have the rest of your family. You have a million things that belonged to your dad—two fucking houses full of his shit." She knew that had been a low blow, but as pissed off as she was right now, she didn't care. There would be time for regret later. "But this ring is the only fucking thing I have left. So do not sit there and tell me you understand what I'm feeling right now."

Anger burned bright in his eyes while she spoke. But he tamped it down by the time she finished, his face so devoid of expression, it looked like he'd had one too many injections of Botox. "I'm trying to protect you," he said in a robotic voice.

"I'm not a damsel in distress, and you can't hide me in a fucking tower!" she shouted, fisting her hands in her hair so hard it hurt. "You've elevated me so high, I can't even see the ground anymore, and I *hate* it. Why can't you get that through your thick fucking head?"

"Eve," he said, his voice infuriatingly low and calm. "I don't think this is a good time to discuss this. We're both too upset. Why don't we take a few minutes to calm down and—"

"Fuck you," she interrupted, eyes narrowing to furious slits. "Don't patronize me."

His face remained deliberately blank, but his hand gave him away. It twitched, as if he longed to take her over his knee and spank her into submission. "I'm not—"

"Yes, you are," she snapped, her gaze homing in on his hand. "And before you get any ideas, emerald. Emerald, emerald, emerald. We are *talking* right now. Nothing else."

Closing his eyes, Jonathan took several deep breaths. "Fine," he said through clenched teeth. He opened his eyes, fixing her with a hard look. "Say what you have to say."

A pair of tears escaped her eyes as she let out a ragged sigh. "I know how hard it's been for you to lose your dad. I'm so, so sorry you're going through that. But you can't use it as an excuse to smother me. I can't *breathe*, Jonathan. You have to let me breathe."

He staggered back two steps, as if the words had been a physical blow to his chest. "What the fuck are you talking about?"

"You literally won't let me go home. When I'm at your house, you won't let me out of your sight. You didn't even let me shower by myself today, for fuck's sake." She ticked off each example on her fingers. "You forced me to go to the hospital against my will. You went behind my back to have that door installed. And now here you are, telling me what I am and am not allowed to do. It's too much, Jonathan. I can't take it anymore."

He blinked at her in what appeared to be genuine dismay. "I'm your Dom," he managed after the silence stretched on for far too long. "It's my job to tell you what you can and can't do."

"In bed," she clarified, over-enunciating both words. "You're my Dom *in bed*. You get to tell me what to do *in bed*. The rest of the time, you're only my boyfriend."

"Only your boyfriend?" For all the understanding on his face and in his voice, she may as well have been speaking in a different language.

For fuck's sake. This was what she got for dating a professional Dom. "I have no interest in dating someone who doesn't let me make my own decisions," she told him, her tone leaving no room for arguments. "I did that shit for sixteen years, and I'm not doing it again. The way you've been treating me since we got back from California . . . it's

161

stopping right now. You need to figure out if you can handle that or not."

Standing there with his mouth hanging slightly open, he stared at her as if she just sprouted a second head. He didn't say a single word.

Her resolve firmed like cement drying, morphing into something unbreakable. If a woman being in charge of her own decisions shocked him this much, this relationship had been doomed from the start. Better to know that now, before she wasted even more of her time.

"I guess you can't," she said, wiping tears from her eyes. "Goodbye, Jonathan." As she turned and walked away from him, dozens of tiny fractures spread through her heart.

CHAPTER 19
Jonathan

The five days after Eve walked out of his life dragged by, minutes seeming to last hours. He spent most of the time in bed, drifting in that space between sleep and awake, barely eating, too hollow to go to work. It felt as if a mild breeze could blow him away if he dared set foot outside his home.

It wasn't until day four that Aiden showed up unannounced in his bedroom. "Enough moping," he said, dragging Jonathan out of bed and into the bathroom.

Even if he wanted to fight, Jonathan didn't have the strength for it. He simply sat on the tiled floor of his shower where Aiden left him, leaning back against the wall as water ran over him. "Please go away," he said, closing his eyes.

"Do you love her?" Aiden demanded, not going anywhere.

"It doesn't matter." He sounded utterly defeated. "Just leave me alone. You have no idea what I'm going through right now."

Aiden scoffed. "I've been here before. Exactly where you are right now. And a very wise man asked me what I just asked you. So fucking answer me, Jonathan. Do you love her?"

"Of course I do," Jonathan snapped, glaring up at his friend through the stream of water.

"Then what the fuck are you doing, man." He reached into the shower, offering Jonathan a hand up. "Get off your ass and go fix whatever mess you made."

Staring at his friend's hand without taking it, Jonathan said, "It's too late for that. She ended it." After a moment, he sighed. "And I deserved it."

"It's only too late if you're not willing to change," Aiden said, the water soaking his sleeve as he kept his arm extended. "Go find her. Tell her you know you fucked up, and instead of giving up, start figuring out how to communicate with each other. It's not going to be easy. You'll need to be completely honest with each other. Vulnerable, even, which I know you fucking hate. But if you don't—if you go through the rest of your life expecting everyone to do as you say, never budging an inch . . ." Sighing, he leaned a little more into the shower, submerging his whole arm in the spray. "It's going to be really fucking lonely, Jonathan. And I don't want that for you."

Communication and honesty.

The words echoed inside his head in his dad's voice. Mere hours before Orson had a heart attack, Jonathan asked him for advice on how to have a real, successful relationship. He'd thought the answer was ridiculously simplistic then. But now . . .

Now he realized how wise his father's advice had been.

Placing his hand in Aiden's, he let his friend pull him to his feet.

Jonathan sat on the wooden bench outside the Fairford Inn three days later. Showered, shaved, and dressed in his favorite suit, he fiddled with his hair, wanting it to be perfect. Everything needed to be perfect.

When at last he decided he couldn't stall anymore, he dug his phone out of his pocket and pulled up his text thread with Eve. "Please say you didn't block me," he murmured as he typed out a whole paragraph of text and hit send, holding his breath until the tiny *Delivered* appeared beneath his message.

Thank fuck. If she'd blocked him, he wasn't sure what his next move would be. Send a letter to the hotel, maybe, and hope she received it.

Two full minutes passed before *Delivered* changed to *Read 11:22AM*. His heart pounded as the seconds ticked by, and he nearly shouted in excitement when three dots appeared, indicating that she was typing out a reply.

His elation didn't last for long. The dots disappeared, reappeared ten seconds later, and then quickly disappeared again. They didn't come back this time.

Fuck, fuck, fuck, he should've included more information. He should've explained everything in the first text. Of course that vague-ass message didn't work.

Before his panic could spiral out of control, he forced himself to close his eyes and focus on his breathing. The message wasn't a mistake, and he knew it.

Though it didn't give the best odds for the result he wanted, it did give Eve the ability to decide if she wanted to give him another chance without being guilted or manipulated into it. After talking it over with Aiden the last two days, he knew that was the most important thing of all. He owed her that.

Even if it broke his fucking heart.

His gaze stayed glued to the phone screen as time marched on relentlessly. Ten minutes passed. Then twenty.

He was preparing to stand when the clock switched over to 11:49. It was over. He'd done all he had any right to do.

That's when the three dots reappeared.

Today 11:20 AM

> I want to talk. But if you don't feel the same way, I understand, and I'll respect your decision. I'm sitting outside your hotel and will wait here for half an hour unless you ask me to leave. If you don't come down, I promise I won't pursue the conversation again. But I'll always be ready to talk if you ever change your mind. No matter how long it takes

Read 11:22AM

> I'll be right down

For several seconds, he couldn't breathe. It worked. It actually fucking worked.

He stood just as Eve stepped out onto the sidewalk. Eyes wary, she watched him as she slowly approached. "What do you want to talk about?" she asked.

"Will you walk down to the coffee shop with me?" he asked, trying to make it clear with his tone that *no* was a perfectly acceptable answer.

"I guess so," she said with a little shrug, falling in beside him as he started down Main Street.

Jonathan longed to reach over and touch her. The urge burned through him like wildfire, setting his nerve endings aflame. To be so close and not feel her smooth skin against his . . . it was a whole new kind of torture.

He shoved his hands in his pockets.

Nothing could keep him from glancing over at her, though. She looked even paler than usual, and he fucking hated it. The vibrant red streaks in her hair had also started to wash out since last he saw her, the resulting color more of a dull orange. It didn't match her spirit in the least. "How have you been?" he asked when she noticed him staring.

Giving him an incredulous look, she said, "Not super awesome. You?"

Yeah, that had been a dumbass question. "Same."

They reached the coffee shop before either of them could think of anything more to say. The words *Bean There, Drank That* were emblazoned across the glass door in a blocky font. A little anthropomorphic coffee bean holding a steaming mug smiled at them from above the shop's name.

Eve eyed the door with the hint of a smile as she pushed it open. "Isn't a coffee bean drinking coffee cannibalism?"

He snorted before he could stop himself. "I would think so." Following her inside, he said, "Why don't you find us a table while I get the drinks."

"I'd rather get my own drink if that's okay." It wasn't a challenge. Just a simple statement of preference.

Resisting the urge to insist he pay for her coffee, he swept an arm toward the counter, letting her go first. He stood behind her, not saying a word as she ordered a medium salted caramel latte to go and paid for her drink. With no choice but to follow her lead, he ordered his iced coffee to go, as well.

A couple of minutes later, they sat at a small, round table by the front windows of the little shop, their untouched drinks sitting between them. Eve watched him with a guarded expression, clearly waiting for him to speak first.

He opened his mouth with every intention of pouring his heart out to her. "I heard through the grapevine that Frank took a plea deal," came out instead, and he resisted the urge to cringe.

Eve arched her eyebrows, but chose not to call him out on his crap. "A five thousand dollar fine," she said with a disappointed shrug. "They gave him the maximum fine, but no jail time since it was technically his first offense."

"That's bullshit," Jonathan said, even though he already knew these details. Zach had told him earlier that morning. Apparently he and Eve still texted every day.

With another, smaller shrug, she said, "Yeah, I'm not thrilled. But at least that guilty plea will be on his record from now on. I'll have to console myself with that." She peered at him over the lid of her cup as she took a sip. "But I don't think that's why you're here."

Okay, enough stalling. "You're right, it's not." Gathering up his shaky courage, he launched into the apology he so carefully prepared the last few days. "First of all, I want you to know that I heard everything you said, and I'm sorry for how I've been acting. I know now that it was a trauma response to my dad passing, which amplified my naturally controlling tendencies. It was an incredibly unhealthy way to act, and I—"

"Okay, therapist Jonathan, calm down," she interrupted, voice caught somewhere between amusement and disbelief. "If we're going to talk, we're going to *really* talk. None of this prepared speech crap."

He gaped at her for a few seconds, then huffed out a small laugh. "Fair enough." Maybe he had gone a little overboard with the therapy speech. "I've been talking to Nell about what happened. She's in the graduate counseling program at the University of Vermont."

The amusement won, and she cracked a smile. "And the world makes sense again."

"She also helped me research grief counselors," he added, needing her to know this part. "I have my first appointment next Monday."

Her smile turned wobbly, and her eyes softened for the first time since she walked out the inn door. "That's great, Jonathan," she said, reaching across the table to squeeze his hand. "I'm really proud of you."

"Did you have any therapy after your dad died?" he asked, curious.

With a little sigh, she shook her head. "I wish. I probably would've done a lot of things differently if I had."

His heart ached at the regret in her voice. "You're only thirty-five," he said, flipping his hand around so he could thread his fingers through hers. "You've got the rest of your life to do things differently."

She squeezed his hand again and didn't pull away. Taking that as a positive sign, he moved on to the next part of his plan. "I have something I want to give you, if you'll let me," he said. "Without agenda or ulterior motive."

"Sounds ominous," she joked, a small smile twitching at the corners of her mouth. "Or like something out of that scene in *Love Actually* where the guy holds up all the signs for Kiera Knightly."

Chuckling, he said, "Nothing ominous. Though I guess it's kind of like that second one."

"He didn't get the girl," Eve reminded him. "Kiera stayed with the other guy."

"And if you don't want to get back together with me, that's okay," he assured her. "I mean it—I'm not doing this to get you back. I'm doing it because I love you, and it's the right thing to do, no matter what."

Eve drew in a sharp breath when he said he loved her. Her eyes searched his—for what, he didn't know.

"I also said that without hope or agenda," he said, hoping he got the wording from the *Love Actually* scene right. Olivia made them all watch that movie at their Christmas party for the last three years. Though he'd never admit it to her, he'd started to look forward to it almost as much as *It's a Wonderful Life*.

For a second, it looked like she would say something. But then she pressed her lips together, like she wanted to keep the words trapped inside. Eyes glistening with unshed tears, she finally pulled her hand out from under his and motioned for him to continue.

Slipping a hand into the inside pocket of his jacket, he pinched the small object there between forefinger and thumb. The pocket's silk lining brushed against his skin like water as he withdrew his hand. Not saying a word, he placed the surprise on the table between them.

She stared at the new ring, confused. "I don't understand."

"I found your emerald, and I took it to a jeweler I know. I told him what you do for work, and he said even after what happened with your dad's ring, a bezel setting is still best." Platinum surrounded the stone on all four sides, holding the emerald securely in place. "The prongs in a more traditional solitaire setting could easily get caught and pry away while you're working, and the last thing I wanted was for you to lose the stone again. As long as you have a jeweler look at it every now and then, they can fix the setting if it starts to wear away."

"Jonathan . . ." Whatever it was she wanted to say, she couldn't seem to find the words. Her gaze stayed glued to the ring on the table.

"He asked me about a thousand questions about you, your personality, your style—everything. Since you hate the only piece of jewelry I've seen you wear, we had to do a lot of guess work on the design."

He'd almost called off the idea right there in the shop, afraid he'd make the already disastrous situation even worse. But the idea of her putting the stone back in the clunky yellow gold ring made it worth the chance. He couldn't let her keep suffering like that.

When she still didn't say anything, he plowed forward, his nerves forcing him to fill the silence. "If you don't love it, the jeweler I used is happy to work with you to make a new design. His name is Theo, and he's easy to work with. I think you'd really like him."

Still nothing out of her, and he was starting to fear he'd fucked up extra big this time.

"Or I can have Theo take the stone out and give it to you. You can put it back in the old ring or whatever you want." He was fucking babbling now, and he knew it. But the words wouldn't stop coming. "If I overstepped here, I'm really sorry. I know how much I fucked up locking you out of that room, and I didn't want you to have to wait any more to get it back. I probably should've given you the stone as soon as I found it, but I wanted you to have a ring that made you happy every time you saw it, instead of one that made you sad. You can—"

"Where was it?" she asked, finally looking up at him.

Oh, thank fuck. He had no idea what had been about to come out of his mouth, but he felt certain it would've haunted him for the rest of his days. "The emerald?" At her nod, he told her, "Under a tile by the tub. I had Theo take all the mortar off. I didn't want to damage the stone."

"But how—" Her voice caught in her throat, and she took a long sip of her coffee as she composed herself. "How did you find it? I don't understand how this is happening right now."

"Lainey showed me how to remove tile. She even loaned me all the safety gear I needed." He shrugged. "Once I got the hang of it, it was just a matter of finding the right tile." Every muscle in his body had ached by the time he caught a glint of green sticking out of dried mortar. His hamstrings and shoulders still fucking hurt, two days later.

She stared at him with wide eyes, her lips forming a small O.

"What?" he asked, trying not to show how much her reaction was starting to freak him out. This wasn't going at all how he'd imagined it in his head—not the perfect scenario where she threw herself into his arms, nor the one where she cursed him out again and disappeared from his life forever.

Still looking thunderstruck, Eve finally managed to say, "You ripped up the bathroom on your own?"

Finally understanding, he had no choice but to look indignant. "I'll have you know, I'm perfectly capable of doing that stuff."

She hid a smile. Very poorly. "That stuff?"

"You know." He waved a hand vaguely, as if that somehow explained everything. "All that Mr. Fix-it, HGTV crap."

"Mr. Fix-it, HGTV crap," she repeated, no longer trying to hide her amusement. "Out of curiosity, before you removed those tiles, when's the last time you held a hammer?"

Jonathan made a show of straightening his tie, belatedly realizing that probably did nothing to help his case. "That's completely irrelevant."

Laughing, she shoved her chair back, hurrying around the table to fling her arms around his neck. "Thank you," she whispered, her breath hot against his ear. "For understanding, for finding it, for the ring—all of it. Thank you so much."

Don't kiss her. Don't touch her. Don't fucking do anything to ruin this. The warning flashed red in his mind, and yet he couldn't help breathing deeply as her sweet lavender scent surrounded him. It felt like gripping a tiger's tail. As long as his tenuous control lasted, he'd be fine.

As soon as it slipped, he was well and truly fucked.

"So, you like the new ring?" he asked, trying to distract them both before the tiger broke free. "Veritas?"

In answer, Eve planted her hands on his shoulders, pushing away just enough so she could look him in the eye. "I love it. I love how much thought you put into it. I love that you found my emerald yourself instead of paying someone else to do it." Plopping down onto his lap, she moved her hands up to cup his face. "I love that you took the time to understand why I was so upset at you, and you're genuinely trying to do things differently now. I love that you talked to Nell and made an appointment with a grief counselor."

Picking up the ring, he slid the delicate platinum band onto the ring finger of her right hand. The light pouring through the coffee shop windows illuminated the emerald, making it look almost magical. The small diamond accents on either side of the large stone shimmered. "That's a lot of love."

"Yes, it is." Leaning forward, she pressed a soft kiss against his lips. "I love that you love me." Another kiss, lasting a little longer this time. "But more than anything, I love *you*, Jonathan. The last week has been complete fucking torture without you."

They both leaned forward at the same time, their mouths colliding with just enough force to hurt. In seconds, they became a tangle of lips and tongues and hands, holding onto each other for dear life as lust and relief crashed over them, combining to make him feel almost lightheaded.

Her tiny whimpers made him regret the choice of Bean There, Drank That for their reunion. If they had just stayed down the street, they could be up to her second-floor room at the inn in under a minute.

The barista coughed loudly, breaking the spell that had temporarily consumed them. "Sorry," Jonathan said, setting Eve on her feet as he stood. Her flushed skin and swollen lips almost dragged him right back under her spell, damn the consequences. But he forced himself to throw a twenty on the table for the poor kid's trouble, and the two practically ran outside, both laughing as soon as the door closed behind them.

"Oh my God, did you see her face?" Eve said, leaning her forehead against his chest as she continued to laugh. "I bet we're permanently banned. They're gonna put our pictures up behind the register and everything."

Jonathan couldn't have kept the grin off his face if his life depended on it. "Worth it," he said, slipping his fingers into her silky hair. He pulled her back so he could look into her eyes as he said this next part. "I know I fucked up, and I'm so sorry. But I'm sure it won't be the last time. I'm going to fuck up again. It's inevitable."

"So will I," she said, eyes full of warmth. "We're only human."

"Exactly." He pressed soft kisses against her forehead, the tip of her nose, and finally her lips. Christ, he loved kissing her. He loved it so fucking much. "As long as we're honest with each other, and we're both willing to talk about it whenever there's a problem, we'll get through it."

One corner of her lips tilted up. "No more control freak stuff?"

He grinned. "I'm not going to make promises I can't keep," he said, laughing when she groaned dramatically. "Christ, can you imagine how crazy I'll be if you ever get pregnant?"

Her breath came out in a little gasp. "Pregnant?"

"You said you always pictured yourself as a mom." He thumbed her lower lip. "And I saw how much you loved playing with my niece and nephews. If that's something you still want—"

"Of course I do." The words came out of her in a rush as wonder filled her eyes. "But do you want to be a dad? Veritas?"

He grinned as her excitement washed over him. "It's not something I really considered before, to be honest. I never thought I'd be in a real relationship, so I assumed it just wasn't in the cards for me. But having a baby with you? Abso-fucking-lutely I want that."

Laughing, she flung her arms around his neck. "God, you make a good point though. You're going to be a horrifying control monster if I'm carrying your child."

"Probably," he admitted. "At least at first. But I promise to try not to, and I'll always keep trying until I get this right. I love you, Evie. I'd do anything in the world for you."

Her smile was absolutely fucking radiant. "I love you, too."

"As long as that part stays true, we'll be able to figure the rest out."

They'd do it together.

EPILOGUE

Eve

Five Months Later

"Shh," Jonathan admonished for the sixth time. "If anyone hears us, I swear to God, you won't be able to sit down for a week."

Eve rolled her eyes. He'd also made the threat six times, and it stopped being scary two iterations ago. "It wasn't even me that time," she whispered back. "It was you." He'd knocked over an empty wine glass someone left on the edge of the stone pathway as they crept through the garden.

He glanced down at the shattered glass at his feet, genuine surprise in his eyes. Light from the three-quarter moon glinted off each jagged fragment, giving it an almost ethereal look. "My apologies," he said after a moment. "Come on."

Hiding an amused smile, she let him lead her through the rest of the garden and across the recently completed front courtyard of the new building. Lainey's crew had put the finishing touches on the courtyard only days ago, finally bringing the expansion project to a close.

That very same day, Lainey had officially offered her a job. She was now second in command at Cox Construction, and they'd start their next project in two weeks, breaking ground on a boutique hotel halfway between Fairford and Burlington. Eve and Jonathan still had a lot of details to figure out, as far as her work travel and living arrangements. But he'd been so damn proud of her when she told him, his eyes glistening with tears as he held her close, that she knew they'd work it all out.

They skirted around the edge of a large fountain in the center of the courtyard. Jonathan and Mason had commissioned a marble statue based on the Botticelli painting *The Birth of Venus*—the goddess of sexual love and beauty emerging from a giant, scalloped shell. Water fell from the sides of the shell into the large fountain basin below.

As they hurried up the front steps to the new building's main doors, Jonathan pulled a large brass key from his pocket. When he inserted it in the lock and tried to turn, however, it didn't budge. Frowning, he tried the handle. The door opened easily, without making a sound.

"Why would it be unlocked?" Eve asked, brows drawing together.

They both looked across the large, opulent entryway to the large double doors beyond. Light crept through the cracks around the doors, standing out like a beacon in the otherwise pitch-black space.

"Who—" she started, but Jonathan held up a hand to stop her.

Taking her arm again, he led her across the cherrywood floors, only listening at one of the ballroom doors for a moment before pushing it open.

"See?" Aiden said as they stepped into the enormous room, voice as smug as his smile. "I told you they'd be along shortly."

Aiden and Olivia stood only five feet farther into the room. Next to them, a nearly naked Nell knelt at Rafe's feet, a thin silver chain dangling between the clamps on her nipples. Two butterfly tattoos decorated her skin—a bright blue and black one on her right thigh, and an even larger one with white and yellow-orange spots on her right hip.

With a sigh, Rafe pulled his wallet from his pocket, took out a hundred-dollar bill, and handed it to Aiden. "That's the last time I bet against you."

Eve did her best to hold back a laugh as Jonathan stared at the quartet, mouth hanging open. Guess they didn't need to do all that sneaking and whispering after all.

"What are you doing here?" Jonathan managed to get out at last.

"Same thing as you, I expect," Aiden said.

Literally bouncing up on her toes with excitement, Olivia added, "Christening the new building before the ceremony tomorrow. Too bad Addison has sharing as a hard limit." The constant up-and-down movement drew Eve's gaze unavoidably to the woman's chest, where her bouncing breasts threatened to tumble out of her low-cut shirt any second. The shirt had to be at least two sizes too small for her and had the words *Daddy's Little Anal Slut* splashed across the front in hot pink text.

For a few more seconds, Jonathan continued to stare at the four already in the room, utterly dumbfounded. Then he threw back his head and laughed. "I should've known," he said, shaking his head. "I bet Leo and Sophie would be here too if they were at the Manor tonight."

Fairford Manor's silent partner and his wife, who lived in Manhattan, planned to arrive by noon tomorrow, in plenty of time for the official ribbon cutting ceremony. Twenty former guests had been handpicked by Jonathan and the others—the first people to ever stay in the new building. The inaugural event in the new space would start with a nine-course meal, followed by a Halloween costume ball.

Banquet tables already filled one end of the room, each set with beautiful champagne-colored tablecloths. Fall-themed floral arrangements sat at the center of each table. Eve couldn't wait to see what the high-ceilinged room would look like once the rest of the preparations had been made.

"So," Jonathan drawled, looking over their accidental gathering. "I see three naughty little girls in this room. I daresay we should do something about that."

Aiden's lips spread into a slow, delighted smile. At the same moment, an almost terrifying intensity flashed in Rafe's dark eyes.

Leading her over to the others, Jonathan deposited her between the other two women. "Stay here," he instructed. The other men gave similar instructions to their partners before the three of them sauntered off toward the tables, speaking low to one another as their footsteps echoed in the cavernous room.

"What do you think they're going to do?" Olivia asked, bouncing up and down with enthusiasm again.

Eve was too excited to answer. *Fucking finally.* In the almost six months of their relationship, he hadn't shared her one single time. Though part of that was her own fault. Since Jonathan had threatened to literally cut off Camden's hand for daring to touch her, it took her a while to build up the nerve to ask. When she had, back at the end of September, he'd promised to set something up soon.

Part of her wondered if it ever would've happened at all if this impromptu gathering hadn't been dumped on his lap. Even when he agreed, he hadn't sounded thrilled by the idea. He would probably always be far too possessive for his own good.

Now it was about to happen, though, she caught that familiar gleam in his eyes—the one that meant he was planning the most delightfully filthy things and couldn't wait to do them to her. She had no idea what had changed.

Deciding to simply count her blessings, she chose not to think too much about it.

"Oh, shit, I think they're ready for us," Olivia whispered, linking her arm through Eve's and turning her around.

Sure enough, after at least two minutes of intense discussion, the men had turned toward them again. Jonathan crooked a finger at them and said, "Come."

Eve and Olivia walked across the ballroom arm in arm, while Nell crawled toward her boyfriend like a panther in heat, brown eyes locked on him the entire way.

By the time the three women stopped a few feet in front of their Doms, Eve's heart raced. She stared into Jonathan's eyes, searching for any hint of what would soon come, but he gave nothing away.

"I've just learned something very interesting," Aiden said, his gaze sliding over each of them in turn. "This will be Eve's first time with more than one partner. Jonathan has been selfishly keeping her all to himself, but he's decided to finally give in to her request and let us all play with her tonight."

Holy fuck, holy fuck, this is happening.

"Aiden and Rafe have promised to make this extra special for you, Evie," Jonathan said, gracing her with a smile that melted her heart. But then the kind, loving look in his eyes turned wicked, and he glanced at the other two women. "And if you two are perfectly behaved and do everything you can to help her through this, Aiden and Rafe will fuck the ever-loving shit out of you afterward."

Olivia pulled her a little closer so she could wrap an arm around Eve's waist, resting a hand low on her hip. "You know I'm fucking in," she said, grinning.

"And you?" Rafe asked, his voice deep and low. "Will you help her?"

"Yes, Sir." Nell's thighs squeezed together as she spoke.

Cupping Nell's cheek with one enormous hand, Rafe murmured, "Good girl."

"The first thing we need you naughty little girls to do is undress Eve for us," Aiden said, gaze raking Eve from head to toe and back. "We want to see our prize for the night."

Soft hands brushed against her skin, setting off goosebumps across her arms and legs. Olivia let her fingernails gently scratch up her sides as she removed Eve's shirt. Not long after, when Nell's fingertips dragged along her hips as she removed Eve's panties, she closed her eyes and shuddered. God, it felt so good.

Once Eve stood naked and exposed, five sets of eyes examining every inch of her, Jonathan ordered, "Now it's your turn. We want all three of you naked tonight."

Olivia pulled off her *Daddy's Little Anal Slut* shirt, then shimmied out of a skirt so short it only covered half of her ass. Her black lace panties and matching bra followed the skirt into the growing pile of discarded clothing. Nell, already naked except for her panties, slid them free of her legs without standing, only lifting her knees and feet far enough off the floor to slide the silky cloth underneath.

Stepping forward, Jonathan cupped Eve's face between both hands, tilting her head up to look at him. "Are you ready?" he asked, voice gentle.

The throbbing ache in her pussy made the answer simple enough to give: "Yes, Sir."

"Good girl. Get on your hands and knees for us."

She slid down to the floor as gracefully as she could, arching her back as soon as she got into position. The smooth, richly colored hardwood was unyielding beneath her, making her knees ache almost instantly. She loved the constant ache of pain.

"You two," Jonathan said, donning his commanding Dom voice at last. "Warm her up for us."

As if she wasn't already dripping down her own thighs.

Nell couldn't have possibly been more enthusiastic as she crawled behind Eve, lapping at her slit like it was a goddamned ice cream cone.

Meanwhile, Olivia shimmied into position under Eve, legs bent at the knees and spread wide. Eve looked down into the brightest blue eyes she'd ever seen. "Kiss me?" Olivia said, breathless with anticipation. It was more a plea than a question.

Dipping her head down, Eve kissed the beautiful woman, moaning as she tasted rich, bitter fruits on her tongue. She had to find out what wine Olivia had been drinking, because she needed this delicious vintage in her life.

Nell started focusing all her attention on Eve's clit, and a few seconds later, Olivia reached up to pinch her nipples, rolling them between her fingers. Fuck, fuck, fuck, this felt way too good. The sensations caused by the two women filled her, beautiful and overwhelming and absolutely fucking everywhere. Moaning again, Eve squirmed, desperate for just a tiny bit more pressure.

So. Damn. Close.

When someone yanked Nell away from Eve's clit, both women shouted their outrage. But as a wide strip of leather slammed down against her ass several times in quick succession, Eve forgot all about her indignance at being edged. Olivia's kiss swallowed up her cry of pain.

"Squeeze as hard as you can," Jonathan ordered from just behind her. Something in her stomach fluttered to learn he was the one wielding the belt.

Olivia gave her nipples the hardest pinch yet, just as Jonathan brought the belt down across her sit spots. Wrenching her mouth away from Olivia's, she cried out at the excruciating pain. This new line of fire hurt more than the other strokes combined.

Before Eve could even think about returning to the kiss, Rafe slid Olivia out from under her, just enough so that the woman's breasts were positioned right below her face. "Suck," Rafe ordered in his low, gruff voice. "Make her feel good."

Lowering herself to her elbows, Eve got to work, taking Olivia's right nipple into her mouth. She sucked on the hard nub, rolling her tongue around it again and again, doing her best to concentrate on the task while Jonathan continued painting her ass red with his belt.

With a deep, ridiculously sexy moan, Olivia buried her hands in Eve's newly dyed hair. The autumn ombre matched the magnificent leaves covering the mountains surrounding the Manor—deep reds and oranges and golden yellows, with a few streaks of emerald green to match her ring.

Panting with the effort of staying still while Jonathan punished her, Eve moved to the other nipple, giving it the same careful treatment as the first.

"Fucking fuck," Olivia said on a gasp. "If you were doing this to my clit, I think I'd literally die. Hint, hint."

Aiden laughed as Rafe dragged Olivia completely out from under her and away. "Naughty little girls who top from the bottom don't get to come, Liv. You know that."

"I'm sorry, Sir," Olivia said, though her pout took something out of the apology. "Please still let me come. I got her ready for you, just like you asked."

"Mmm." Aiden walked lazily around his wife. "I'll consider it."

Olivia started to beg, but Eve didn't hear anything else they said. The belt snapped against her sit spots twice more, the loud *crack* of leather against skin echoing in the room. Her scream carried through the double impact, and every muscle in her body shook as she pressed her forehead against the floor.

"You're such a good girl," Jonathan said, moments before he dropped the belt. The heavy silver buckle hit the hardwood with a dull *thunk*. "Are you ready for us to fuck you now?"

Words completely failing her, all she could do was moan in response.

Jonathan knelt behind her, and she felt the head of his cock press at the entrance to her pussy. "Be still," he ordered when she tried to push back, giving her hip two quick swats.

"Time to get up," Rafe growled from above her, hauling her back up onto her hands.

Her arms trembled, almost too weak to hold her up. Locking her elbows, she tilted her head back as far as she could.

Rafe already unbuckled his own belt and dark jeans, and she looked up just in time to see him pull his enormous cock free. "Jonathan tells me you love to have a cock shoved down your throat," he said, kneeling in front of her. The head brushed against her lips. "Open, little one."

Spreading her lips as wide as she could, she waited, breathless, for it to finally happen. Two men at once, both so goddamned beautiful it almost hurt to look at them. Jesus fuck, how had her life changed so much so fucking fast?

Jonathan must have given Rafe a signal, for they pushed into her simultaneously, maddeningly slow but unrelenting. Squeezing her pussy as tight as she could, she swirled her tongue around Rafe's cock—wetting, sucking, preparing for his inevitable invasion of her throat.

He bumped against the back of her throat as Jonathan bottomed out inside her. She tried to relax her muscles, to let him in, but she needed more time. Sucking him as hard as she could, she hummed, loving the jerk of his cock at the vibration.

"You may be able to distract me for a minute," Rafe ground out, his hands gripping her hair. "But your reprieve won't last long. You *will* let me in."

Both men began pumping in and out of her, still so slow it made her want to scream with impatience. She didn't want them to give her time to acclimate. She wanted to revel in the pain as they took what they wanted, whether she was ready for them or not.

A pair of long, delicious moans drifted over her. She'd been so caught up in what Jonathan and Rafe were doing, she completely forgot about the other three.

The next time Rafe pulled most of the way out of her mouth, she caught a glimpse of Nell and Olivia, spread out on top of one of the banquet tables. Aiden was hard at work, fucking them both with his fingers.

Fuck, that was hot. Though one of them better remember to change the tablecloth in the morning, or Remy would likely kill them all.

Her distraction ended as quickly as it began. Rafe finally didn't stop when his cock nudged against the back of her throat. He kept pushing, pushing, holding her head in place as she worked to loosen her throat muscles.

"Good girl." Rafe said it on a moan as he slipped deeper inside her, his cock disappearing into her mouth. The next time he and Jonathan pulled almost completely free, he said, "She's ready."

Their restraint clearly on a hair trigger, they both surged forward so hard and fast, she half expected to crumple like an aluminum can. Holy fucking shitballs, it hurt so fucking good. Tears welled in her eyes as they fucked her from either end, fast and hard and glorious.

Lifting one leg, Jonathan planted his foot beside her, his hard thigh rubbing against her hip with each pounding stroke. The new angle made her gasp around the cock in her mouth. Holy fuck, if he could just do that—

Again. And again. And a-fucking-gain. *Holy fuck, holy fuck . . .*

Pulling out of her mouth at the last second, Rafe pumped his cock with his hand, emptying himself onto her chest. Her breasts bounced with every thrust from behind as Rafe covered her with his seed.

She closed her eyes as Rafe's come began dripping onto the floor. It was too much—all way too much. This had been a mistake. She wouldn't survive this. It would burn her up from the inside with its scorching heat.

Only one, two, three more thrusts, and then she was falling—tumbling so hard and fast into the abyss as colors exploded behind her eyelids.

Too much, too much, too fucking much.

Jonathan roared behind her as he came, his fingers digging into her hips with bruising force. The pain brought her back to herself just as another wave of pleasure shot through her with the speed of a bullet, leaving her utterly breathless.

By the time they were both spent, Eve felt like she was floating ten feet in the air. Only Jonathan's near-scalding touch as he gathered her into his arms brought her back down to planet Earth.

"You were incredible," Jonathan praised, stroking her multi-colored hair while Aiden and Rafe descended upon the other women. "I've never seen anything more beautiful and perfect in my life."

Practically purring with delight, she watched as Rafe bent Olivia over the table with the ruined tablecloth, wrapping her long, dark hair around his fist. Bending her head back so far she'd probably need a fucking chiropractor by morning, he pounded into her from behind.

By the time her gaze drifted sleepily toward the other two, Nell was back on her knees. "Fuck yourself with your fingers," Aiden demanded as he drove into her mouth over and over. The beautiful woman moaned, two fingers sinking into her dripping pussy with a loud, wet sound.

"How is this even real?" she murmured, the words slurring slightly like she was drunk.

Chuckling softly, Jonathan planted a kiss on the top of her head. "This is only the beginning, Evie. I've got so much more to show you."

Her eyes drifted closed, and she smiled. She couldn't fucking wait to see what he had planned next.

The End

Acknowledgments

Let me start by saying that this book was extremely hard for me to write. Not because of the story itself, which I love with all of my heart. But because my life imploded in a lot of ways earlier this year, and it took me several months to put the pieces back together. I'm endlessly grateful for the people who responded to multiple missed deadlines with kindness and patience.

Karen Washo, you are one of the kindest people I know. Thank you so much for understanding as I kept pushing the schedule back and back and back. You continue to be the greatest editor I could possibly hope for, and I'm so proud of this story you helped me create. Thank you, from the bottom of my heart, for everything you do for me.

Thank you, also, to Linda Russell at Foreword PR & Marketing for your patience and understanding as I worked my way through the struggles of this year. Having you and your team in my corner makes this whole indie publishing thing seem possible, no matter how impossible everything else in my life might feel. I know I've said it before, but I'd be lost without you guys.

I didn't think I'd ever have a cover more stunning than the butterfly on the Book 2 paperback, but holy guacamole. The emerald on this paperback cover still makes my eyes go wide every time I see it. The green on both covers has seriously been giving me life since the moment I saw the proofs. Since people absolutely do judge books by the cover, I'm so glad I get to work with someone as prodigiously talented as Robin Johnson at Florida Girl Design.

Virginia Carey, you continue to be the most brilliant of proofreaders. Thank you for always catching my little mistakes. I promise you that sometime before I die, there will come a day when I remember that *bow tie* is two words, not one . . . but it unfortunately wasn't this day.

Thank you, thank you, thank you to Shari Ryan at MatHat Studios, who once again did a brilliant job formatting both versions of this book. All my books are truly a thing of beauty because of your skills, and I'll never get over being able to hold something so perfect—*with my name on the cover*—in my hands. Four novels and two novellas in, and it's all still surreal as hell.

To all the people who worked with me to come up with the right name for Eve, I literally couldn't have done this without you. Taryn, Kelly, and Rachel, your input is so very appreciated. To the hilarious bartender whose name I can't remember, who came up with Eve/Evie, if I see you again, I'll leave you an extra big tip. Also, you make the best custom cocktails of all time. All right, who am I kidding. It's a Friday night. Time for nachos and cocktails, baby.

And finally, Jason. You're my favorite human being on the whole planet, and I wouldn't be able to do any of this without your endless love and support. I'm so grateful to have you as the other half of my team. I love you as big as the whole universe.

Also by Bay Sinclair

Fairford Affairs

Fixing Olivia

Unravelling Nell

Savoring Addison

Fairford Affairs Novellas

Rewarding Sophie

Liberating Zach

About the Author

Bay Sinclair is the author of steamy romance with broken girls, sexy Doms, and lots of heart. She writes contemporary romance—though she was one credit away from a history minor in college, and historical romances hold a special place in her heart. When she isn't writing, she's an avid foodie in search of the next great culinary adventure, and she drinks entirely too much green tea.

Connect Online
BaySinclair.com